5 Short Stories

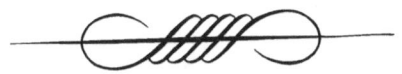

5 Short Stories

Steve April

c/o POB 4475
Mountain View, CA 94040-0331

First Printing
ISBN #978-0-9744686-6-2

A Barberry Book

Also By Steve April

Poetry
Poet In California
The Unicorn And The Prom Queen
The Einstein Club
The Weavers
The Sunflower
Scenes From Law School

Birds In America

Fiction (Novel)
Detour

To Maxine, again

Contents

Preface

The Hunger. A Bay Area coming of age story, restless hearts seeking unity. The universe is a new-sprung flower, needing water. Begun in my 30s, revised 25 years later.

Joseph's Story. A sanctuary story, a journey across the river Styx, with subterranean emotional turmoil, and mind-vision fireworks, opening into a three-way relationship, a "retreat" that starts a hip, new life hopefully.

The Bridge. A story with a "suspect" narrator, um delicious. Is he trustworthy? Reliable? Or a psychopath? You decide, dear reader.

Those Who Wait. A new cinema course, and "Bible As Literature" university course opens into the surreal, grounded, however, with vivid details, and old-fashioned storytelling, in a kind of new wave apotheosis. Written in my 20s, revised many years later.

No Way Out. A spontaneous little bop, based on witnessing an event in a restaurant, written in my 20s.

1
The Hunger

It was Sunday. The clock struck an hour on the morning side of twelve. Many of the families that make up our great country display their thanks and piety at mass, at such an hour. Hardworking, prosperous fathers, in the well-to-do communities lead their well dressed wives, or fashionable, cool wives, to whose expensive skirts two or three little children cling, proudly and ceremonially to the great bronze doors, standing beside before their entrance, and making way. The sermon crowns the mild theatrics and the fragrant mysteries of the service. The inspirational organ resounds through the high vaults promoting the lofty and enlightening sermon. The strains of this powerful instrument echo through the week for the lucky, blessed churchgoing families at work or home or school. Likewise the spirit of the service colors their rounds in society, promotes their peace with nature, society and God. Their world is limited and comprehensible and almost kind, the world of the well-to-do. Even business' much accoladed cut-throat aspects are cut-throat according to rules, and the chances of feeling the wrath of the blade decline if one keeps one's nose to the grindstone.

But the bells also ring on the other side of town. And another congregation gathered this Sunday morning in the bus station, not so privileged or well-to-do. In all directions they were coming and going, amid their dramas, perhaps to visit relatives, or friends, and of this congregation a few had degenerated and disintegrated, or were involved in such a process, to extremes.

Katrina Johansson stretched to relax, til the baggage man laid out the suitcases, and she strode over to the pile, and picked her own. She made her way through the glass doors, among scores of others, past a popcorn machine, and a snack stand. Beyond this, and to the left lay the ticket windows, and straight ahead the doors. The doors to the world at large! The gates to the city! The city where somewhere Debbie played her games and went to school. How close she was, on the verge of thrusting out into her new life. She had only to walk through the doors to begin. But she could not, not yet, as most of her fellow travelers made to the door with a light step. Rather she stood against the rail bordering the lobby dabbing at her eyes with her handkerchief, and taking big breaths.

The lobby consisted of plastic, pastel seats bolted down by rows. A portion of the seats had big TV screens attached that operated on insertion of a quarter. At one of these, there was an elderly man with broken teeth huddled in a sodden coat, gumming a donut. In another, a drunken Indian caressing a wine bottle with his cheek and singing an old song; a runaway sat in another watching TV and waiting for her connection. Such were the ones who seemed to have little left to lose, for whom a twisted past spoke darkly of a bleaker future.

A couple of this kind, two men in shabby overcoats arguing over their paper bag, lurched from the coffee counter, towards the lobby along the aisle where Katrina stood blowing her nose.

The first had a leathery greenish tinge to his skin, bloodshot, ferocious eyes, and sensual, slavering lips. His companion had thick lips under which was revealed big, brown teeth, black, greasy hair, and a seven day beard, framing mean little eyes, that spit malign dislike. These two confronted a newbie in town, this young woman in the aisle, Katrina.

The fellow with the lizard-like mien roared, "you're blocking the way, you foolish girl. Do you think that your tears have significance here? Everybody comes here, don't imagine that you're better than the rest. Get out of the way, for I have been known to tread a person down, like a beetle in the dust." He brandished a bottle mightily over his head, and then treated himself to a rapacious swig on second thought. "Yeah, yeah, you're blockading the path, you dumb girl you," his friend chimed, taking up the thread. "We ain't no church-mouses here. We know your dirty thoughts, you stupid girl. Hurting your poor old mother, are we? Come with us, we'll show you a good time, girlie, we will."

The Lizard-y guy moved closer to put his arms around Katrina. His companion's ribald laughter egged him on to fury at this stolid, immovable girl, who refused to budge.

Henry Deville was working on the second floor, in the administrative offices, on assignment. When he heard the commotion, curiosity drew him to the rotunda, where he surveyed the scene.

Not that the patrons were disinterested or deaf. A wife's mandatory restraining hand on the arm of her balding husband canceled what appeared to be an imminent impulse to rise to the girl's rescue. A couple of swarthy women gathered their children in their arms, and turned their heads from the disreputable accosting. Another woman sitting there, turned to look, eyes glittering with malevolent mirth. A middle-aged man with a cheap suitcase regarded the two drunks distastefully, but watched with helpless fascination as he waited for departure. The juveniles by the snack machines regarded the scene intently, and acted as if this were a scene from a romantic play.

"Hey, leave her alone," Henry meddled in between them. "Get lost, before I bash your head against the wall," he exclaimed. He gave the Lizard a light shove.

"Get lost you. I'm tired of creeps like you that imagine you can harass me and get away with it," exclaimed Katrina, taking heart at Henry's appearance, and finding her tongue.

"These gentlemen friends won't last," the Lizard exclaimed, and twisted, after tumbling back from Henry's intercession, and regarding her with a baleful eye. "Ten years from now girlie, where will you be? You're too good for us but not your gentlemen friends, but you'll see by and by, wait and see, have no fear."

"Go back to your mother," the other piped. "Before it's too late, mend the error of your ways. You've caused your dear mother so much pain and grief. Your gentleman friend wants only one thing, stupid girl. Go home, before you get caught up with the red lights and all, you are headed for a life of sin, and you will be punished good, in the end, you will," he continued.

"Look here, you rogues, you noisesome, boisterous sods," Henry exclaimed, cocking a fist as the second man leaned in with his defaming accusations. Should he bust a bridge on the Lizard's nose, or go for the other's sagging belly?

"You bastards," said Katrina. "What do you know, don't tell me what to do," she exclaimed furiously, and stamped her feet. She looked like a tawny cat, stamping her feet, thought Henry. "Oh, oh, here we go," cautioned Henry, talking to himself.

The two characters finally withdrew without a sign of fear from Henry's threats, or her words, however. They didn't care, as if they had charged their conscience with such abuse they hadn't a remainder to retreat in shame, as if they had charged their bodies with such degradation, that the normal measures of pain had shriveled so that the prospect of a physical pounding held no terror. They tossed off drinks, retreating and remarking, "you'll see us here, not too far gone, and you'll be asking us for drinks, that day, you will, and we won't have nothing for you girlie, no we won't."

"Never nothin' for nasty girls like you," the other roared, flashing his teeth. And slowly they made their way out the door, into the city.

The drunks staggered towards the door, and the street. The spectacle concluded, one of the husky women released the children who flew about the room like little moths; the tough guys in black jackets looked for further entertainment in the direction of the runaway who began powdering her nose; a couple balding, middle-aged men continued to look in her direction admiring her build, holding their coffee, and the would-be rescuer and wife returned to their TV.

"Wow, I'm glad we got rid of them," Katrina exclaimed forcefully. She refused Henry's offer to shepherd her suitcase with a stubborn shake of her head. "You helped me out of a jam. Which way to the Y?"

They entered the teeming world of Sunday urban sprawl. Katrina seemed totally different now. Her powers returned swiftly, she put those men behind her, turning to Henry for guidance.

Katrina Johansson was a young woman in her early twenties. She had a tentative, even dazzled demeanor, but there was an air of resilience in back of it. She was ready for adventure, thought he, amid 100 desolations and 100 loves, was ready to make her break, with dauntless expectations and shiny eyes.

Katrina looked like a winner. Katrina's thrusting, dauntless chin, and strong, sensual mouth, with fleshy lips like fruit, combined with her sturdy shoulders and rippling back, the back of a Valkyrie, as much as a mermaid, contributed to this impression. She had a back that could hold up the world. Her most remarkable feature was her hair—a fine, honey-blonde growing thick and cut short so that with her strong walk and proud demeanor Katrina might have brought to mind in the spectator happily observing her entrance into her new life a tawny cat.

But something was amiss with this tawny cat, there came suddenly tears into her eyes, dancing grey-green eyes that sparkled like cappers, she trembled and put down her suitcase amid the rackets and the grinding of the street, and pulled a handkerchief superbly from a little blue purse she carried in her free hand. Having accomplished this maneuver, she thereupon blew her nose loudly and resolutely, after which she took a deep breath or maybe two, straightened her shoulders smartly, and shook herself (like a wet dog), before rejoining her rescuer.

A philosopher by nature and a joker by disposition, Henry observed this tawny cat (young lady) blowing her nose and thought, "she's come here prepared for adventure with great verve and enthusiasm. But she is in eclipse, she is like a gifted race-car driver haunted by a recent accident. What circumstances could have conspired to create this sorrow? I'm going to try and find out."

Henry was a tall, lean fellow. He had a slightly aquiline nose, and a close-cropped thick, dark head of hair, an olive complexion, and lustrous eyes. Many races mingled in his blood. He congratulated himself heartily for doubling back, and he turned these eyes like beacons on the young lady, and much to his surprise, received a brief flare of recognition, before her eyes sought the street. He felt encouraged by this flare of recognition and launched spontaneously into a little speech.

"I think you're beautiful," he said. "But these days that's not enough. It's tough out there. What attracts me is something else entirely, dare I confess! Look our handkerchiefs, they match," he exclaimed, thrusting a large blue and red handkerchief indeed resembling her own, into the air. He continued, replacing his handkerchief, "I've never seen such a beautiful lady blow her nose like that, I'm totally disarmed and charmed. Look, you're new in town, and I've got a few hours. You're hungry, I'm sure. Why don't we get lunch and I'll show you around," he suggested easily. "This is a beautiful city, and I'll consider this my civic duty to adjust the wrongs done by the noisesome drunks. What do you say?"

"There's the Golden Gate Bridge, Fisherman's Wharf, Union Square, the De Young museum, North Beach, with their well know eateries, there's Yerba Buena Gardens, the

Exploratorium, the San Francisco symphony, to name a few. There's Lombard Street, the crookedest little street in the world, so called, there's the Cliff House and Seal Rock, where the seals bask all hours, while the surf pulses in. Very slippery, beware."

"If it's not out of your way," replied Katrina cautiously. "I wouldn't want to put you out." But her face lifted to his like a flower to sunlight.

"Not at all, you want to get to the Y, right?"
She nodded.

"Okay, we'll go eat and I'll guide you to the Y, how's that? Put a little pep into your first day. There's a nice little diner a few blocks away."

"Sounds great. I'm so hungry I could eat a horse."

"Where are you from?" asked Henry, after they'd made their introductions, and the couple directed themselves north at Henry's gesture. Foggy Sunday. Liquor stores, transient hotels, and a big gray courthouse. They passed a few women with squalling boys, and men in shabby raincoats.

"Topeka," she responded, suitcase banging against her leg, proceeding gamely. "I've come to get my kid," she said with a resolution, simultaneously morose, and ferocious.

"Oh you have a kid, hey that's swell, so do I."

"Debbie," replied Katrina. "I'm divorced," she informed him after a moment's hesitation. "My ex-husband's got custody. I've come to get my baby back."

"Oh, my daughter's name is Daisy Jane. I'm divorced too. I see her on the weekends," said Henry glibly. "Gee, what a coincidence."

What a coincidence indeed! The delightful occasion of their mutual single parenthood being established they pressed on, Katrina noticeably more relaxed, and Henry electric with delightful affability, and the decorous diplomacy of the tour-guide.

The sun broke through the fog occasionally, an erratic swordsman, and briefly colored the streets and buildings golden. Katrina could make out flashes of water between a building, far in the distance, as they walked from the slummy neighborhood, into a shopping district which this Sunday morning however, boasted sparse patronage.

There was something about him that concerned her; his scowling, almost wolfish intensity; and something likewise that attracted her; a luminous boyishness, and glimpse of humor breaking through often. Henry stood much taller than her; that too intimidated her.

"How old is Debbie?"

"Six now. She had a birthday recently."

"And you missed it, shame on you," Henry teased.

"Well, I've been in a nut-house, as they say," Katrina replied, wincing at his comment. "Courtesy of my husband, my responsible husband, basically."

"A nut-house, God," Henry replied horrifically. "You poor baby. That must have been awful," he sympathized.

Katrina responded airily, waving her hand, "don't ask."

"Young mother, what's your philosophy on parenting?" Henry switched gears, amid the silence, while they walked briskly, breathing in the misty air.

If at an impasse, they could talk about their children.

"Are you of the school of thought that kids are *tabula rasa*? You know, blank slates, basically an animal, with instincts, that need guidance and training. Or do you lean more to the notion that children are like plants, and as plants need water, nurturing and loving function essentially like rain, and they trail clouds of immortality, like the bard said?"

"I'm aware," responded Katrina, "that the human factor's more important than a philosophy, especially an inflexible view. Love's the key. And education. Of course, there are times children should be disciplined, and they do need guidance naturally. My childhood was mortifying a good part of the time. I grew up in an accusatory atmosphere, with my parents squabbling constantly. I got accused of crimes I did not commit. That's a terrible burden. I was a gloomy child, and I'd hate to do to Debbie what my parents did to me."

"Well spoken, young lady," Henry affirmed. He was liking her. "Who did the accusing, your mother, your father?"

"Children are so impressionable and malleable, they play the role their elders require them to play, at times," she responded vaguely. "I've been playing a role, plugged into this role, most of my life. I've got to leave it behind, and grow. Until I shuck it like a mask, an outworn mask, will I even be a fit mother?"

"You've come here to put your life together, to get back on your feet and start anew," Henry declared warmly. "This is a place of new beginnings, folks come all over the world to do this."

"Where's the diner?" asked Katrina anxiously, "up the block on the right," replied Henry, "don't worry. You're putting your best foot forward, and you are determined to succeed. But what are you talking about, what role?" Henry insisted impatiently. He wanted the details, the elements of her complaint, and source of distress.

Why couldn't she say what was on her mind? Men tended to be straightforward. Why did woman have to be opaque, and mysterious?

"The role of a victim," Katrina replied hoarsely, in a new tone.

Henry turned and caught in her countenance a dreamy look, out of which tears volatilized briefly, until she rapidly blinked a few times, and shut down the painful, dreamy fountain with a dazzled blank look, straightening her shoulders resolutely. "Those men at the station," she continued. "They picked me out, it's an instinctive thing. They knew I'd crumble when I did, stay paralyzed. They latched onto me. But it's not important now," she trailed off.

"On the contrary," replied Henry, "they were a couple of stumblebum drunks, and you happened to be there. Don't go around making up harmful myths about yourself, for goodness sake. Save your strength for recovering, don't spend energy beating yourself up," Henry urged, with friendly insistence in his eyes.

"You don't understand," Katrina emphasized, "but it doesn't matter. Don't know why I brought it up, except we were talking about our children, and one should be aware, I feel, how the practices of a prior generation get planted like seeds in the next, and learn from history, or one is doomed to repeat the errors of the previous generation."

This winding sentence fell from Katrina's mouth like a ripe plum, a textbook exercise, and appeared to Henry to directly contradict the spirit and the letter of Katrina's previous statement how she was actively working on shucking her mask, her role. The expression in her eyes went remote and dreamy and contrasted markedly with the textbook tone, Henry observed.

"I bet that you're hungry after that long ride. We're coming up to my little restaurant. Here we are," Henry informed her, holding the door for her.

"I'm starved," Katrina replied gracefully. "I could eat a horse."

The waitress came up and gave them a smile, and they followed her past the counter and kitchen on the right, and took a middle booth made out of dark wood. Colorful pictures of the circus hung on the wall, clowns, elephant riders, and lion tamers. The waitress, a plump brunette, dropped down their menus, and when she returned Henry ordered an omelet stew, and Katrina ordered blueberry pancakes and coffee.

Henry felt that they stood poised on the lip of establishing a wonderful connection. Contrary to discouraging him, though her story offered trap doors also, she intrigued him. She appeared enigmatic and mysterious, a self-contained secret being, with secret joys and sorrows, secret hopes and vendettas. There was, also, something generous about her dazzled river look, like she had stepped off from a kayak, there were suns and futures as well as moons and eclipses, she had a dazzling grace, like the daughter of a shaman, at

16

home in many elements.

He felt a desire to get to know her better, to bring their lives into the same orbit. He had rescued her, and felt heroic around her, in contrast to his self-image these days. They both had children too, daughters at that, which was a great common bond. But he had to be careful, for if he did not follow the proper path, all might be lost, and quickly.

"We're beautiful, perfect strangers, bits of cosmic fire flickering as we cruise by, hey Tom Cruise, and for all we know have but one life to live, so I'll tell you there are three main issues in my life, such as it is. Love, family, and work. And a word sums up all three and my world these days; frustration," declared Henry, a bit histrionically.

"I found out how love and work are connected, when my wife left me, after I quit my stockbroker career, and took a break. Well, got laid off actually, due to downsizing. So I gave culinary school a try, and my wife up and left, and took Daisy Jane with her, naturally. Graduated, and became a chef at a nice establishment, but they fired me, so I worked as a short order cook for awhile. I felt desolate. I felt like I was driving a car, with busted headlights on a pitch black night, and hit a wall. So I turned the thing around and drove in the opposite direction, and hit a wall. Took computer courses at a community college, and got into software, coding, all that. I'm beginning to wonder if life isn't this cumulative breaking and bashing against these two walls, until one's an utter wreck emotionally," he exclaimed. "A few good friends help, thank goodness. But Daisy Jane, she's my sunlight, my freedom. I love my daughter with a passion."

He looked about him, thought Katrina, with bright,

shiny eyes, at the waiters talking by the counter, the cook visible at the grill, the doo-dads, a bear on a tree stump, scattered about. A large Wurlitzer played a diverse selection of music, from many eras, a nice touch.

"Are you interested in hearing this?" he leaned forward abruptly, clasping her hands. To her amazement she did not pull away immediately, and merely detached his hand from hers. She felt his friendly eyes imploring her, like a mild heat, his imploring face. She decided that she liked him, despite he scared her a little.

"Tell me about your family," she replied, with a tight little smile. "We'll swap tales. Go ahead."

"Well, families are the center of one's gravity, until one blasts off," he labored to articulate. "I wonder how much frustration and contravened impulse could be attributed to this." As he talked his hands rested inches from hers. He had big, bony hands with beautifully tapering fingers, the hands of a hunter, the fingers of a musician.

"My dad's a sailor. He'd be around about six months a year, when I was a boy. He was a charming, charismatic guy. When I was nine, the day before my ninth birthday, when I ran home from school so happy he was home, that's when he left. Left my mother and brother and me, walked out to get booze one night, and never returned. My mother could not help but be pulling at us, she had only us to love. My mom loved him and he left her destitute and broken-hearted. My mom's father, a banker, stepped in, played the father figure, to a degree. God, what fantasies I had in connection with my father, and how I hated him for leaving us. My mother died a couple years ago, from breast cancer. And you know

18

that bastard had the gall to ring me up a month or so ago. Wanted to get back in touch. That bum, I hope he burns in hell."

Henry's eyes seemed smoky and hot, thought Katrina.

"What a guy," she replied sympathetically.

Katrina had a mixed reaction to her impromptu guide. On the one hand, he harangued her, in a thoughtful way. On the other hand she felt a boyishness in back of his critical, judgmental imploring, albeit an embattled boyishness. And coated in heat, his words reached her, boyish and fiery with suppressed ardor, though he talked morosely.

"But I've run on enough," he smiled weakly, as the food came, looking rather annoyed with himself. "I like hiking, camping. Pt. Reyes, Mt. Tam. I could take you..."

The waitress smiled and urged on them a good repast and they dug in. They both ate heartily, he stopping, wolfish and avid, occasionally to observe her putting away her meal, and returning enthusiastically to his.

"So tell me about you," he urged after awhile.

"As for love," said Katrina, "I don't know what that means except—I love my daughter for sure," she lilted superbly. "Marrying got me out of my parent's house, looking back, which I had to do. He stuck me in a nut-house when he came home and found me drunk out of my mind a couple times with Debbie—for certain reasons..." and she tossed him a look as if to say which will remain undivulged. "Debbie's my life, man. I've got to get her back. I'm gonna hire myself a lawyer and get her back."

"As for my family, I don't want to talk about them," she declared.

"Enough of me. Go on," he encouraged.

"As for work—I'm terrified—I haven't worked in six years, but I'll do it for Debbie, 'cause I need an income. My husband had a macho attitude, did not want me to even look for work, though being a salesman at a car dealership, he'd often come home angry. They were always on the verge of layoffs there, also, so it seemed. For Debbie, I'm gonna work and save. I want to get a nice little job, and save some money. I have to—I need a lawyer, and lawyers are expensive."

Henry looked around at a few of the customers. An Asian couple sat at a booth, mother at work feeding her little tot, while the child exhibited a seeming animosity to an omelet. In another booth two well-coiffed women sat, pearls gleaming, and the back of the other woman's heads bobbing like a metronome. Perhaps from the beauty parlor, visible outside the window.

They ordered a refill, and when their waitress returned and laid down the check, she declared, "hi, my name's Donna. A pleasure to serve you today. I couldn't help overhearing that you were looking for a job."

Donna proceeded to explain how Gary, the owner, the guy by the grill with the mustache, needed help, and invited Katrina to talk to him about it.

Katrina looked to Henry for guidance and he declared, in an encouraging tone, "go for it."

Thus encouraged, Katrina took her characteristic deep breath, and removing her suitcase to exit the booth, pushed it back on Henry's side, and went over to the counter. She came back a couple of minutes later with tears in her eyes.

"I've got the job," she declared, amazed.

Donna came and served them refills and Katrina thanked her profusely for the heads-up, and invited her to sit. "You seemed nice and I could tell that you just got into town," said Donna, as two diners made their entrance. "I got here four months ago myself," she explained. "I'll see you Monday," she declared, rising to tend to them.

"Wow, first day in town and she's got a gig. Wish I could get jobs that easy," Henry teased. "This one's on me," he reassured her, perusing the check. He left a very nice tip. Katrina, with gratitude, added to the pot.

Katrina waved to the manager and Donna as they left and exclaimed, "Oh, I'm so scared—but Debbie—for Debbie I'll do it."

Katrina gestured to a distant ship from the top of a hill, as they began a descent and Henry nodded, "yeah, I was in the Merchant Marines a couple of years."

"Oh, really," Katrina exclaimed. "How wonderful. Do tell."

"Not a bad gig," Henry declared neutrally. "You get to travel. New faces, new places. You can go to sleep in Taiwan and wake up in Hong Kong. One gets breasted by the waves. A lot of sights and cultures."

"Sounds exciting," Katrina exclaimed. Her bright, sunlit face lit up at the notion.

"Was this before or after you were a stockbroker?" she wondered.

"After. Before, I fancied myself a writer in my early days. I took the training program, and got myself a place on a ship."

"Sounds so exciting, and romantic," ventured Katrina,

her eyes cast over the water, observing the ship. "I'd love to go to sea for a year."

"Yeah," said Henry noncommittally. "You can go around the world, round and round, but yourself you can't go around," he added after a brief pause. "Wherever you go, there you are. I'd miss my daughter, been a landlubber every since."

At a Civil War statue midway down the hill, a gaggle of tourists greeted them cheerily, and before they knew it, each pose for pictures in front of the statue, the kids laughing merrily. They were from Sweden. The kids ran about like hatters; they jumped up and down in the air like loons; they pulled big faces; the grown ups also; the tots laughed and capered; the wife smiled; and the Swede clicked an apotheosis, they'd become a part of the landscape.

"Ah, spring is in the air, there's a fresh breeze blowing through these streets, the flowers are leaning to the sun, we want to enjoy, and live. Beside these stern edifices, stirred mayhaps by an ocean breeze, in their corners little flowers peep, see," Henry exclaimed, and he pointed out a popping of yellow gardenias in the dappled shade of an apartment building. "The soil rouses itself from its slumbers, I've been waiting so long. Here's for you," he declared and jumped the picket fence with a spry leap, picked some pretty yellow blossoms, and thrust them in her hand.

"I've been waiting, I feel the sea and the flowers mingle, it's a delicious scent," Katrina exclaimed heartily, accepting the token with a blush.

"What ho, what ho," they heard and turned to witness a procession cross the street. Six or eight little people crossed the street. Katrina thought it was a child's masquerade party but her impression foundered on closer inspection. "Hey, midgets," Henry exclaimed.

"Not midgets, sir," the spokesman strode up, confronting him sternly, and admonishing his slip with a raised finger. "We are the little people representing the *Little People's Circus*, and we're selling tickets to our show next week. Care to purchase tickets? This show will amaze and astound all lovers of humanity and animals with its death-defying feats. See the courage, the sacrifice, the derring-do of the little people as they battle tremendous odds and challenge the very bounds of propriety and the laws of nature," he said in a carny voice.

"Delighted, delighted," Henry exclaimed. "Very pleased to meet you," exclaimed Katrina demurely.

Greetings being made all around, one by one the fantastic figures stepped up and shook the pair's hands, posing in their most professional, fantastic poses. The spokesman was so overjoyed with Katrina's and Henry's manifest enthusiasm that he introduced the members spontaneously, like a ring-master, and they proceeded to commit deeds representative of their line of work.

"Here's Boudine, the sword-swallower," the ringmaster proclaimed in a carny voice. "A tiny tot deserted on the deserts of Great Arabia. He stowed away on an oil-tanker and joined up in Des Moines. His claim to fame is the greatest little sword-swallower in the world," the ringmaster exclaimed.

Boudine, the sword-swallower, with a gravelly greeting, saluted the pair. He wore black britches and a flaming yellow shirt and a great, cocked hat with a feather. A little lady produced a two foot sword, and slowly he lowered the sword into his mouth, inch by painful inch. Halfway plunged, inch by inch the brave sword-swallower brought the steel up, from his pint-sized maw, face to the sky.

"He'll swallow it up to the hilt if you come see our show," the ringmaster boasted, as Boudine, bowing with a great flourish and doffing his feather hat stepped aside.

"Next," the ringmaster declared, "Gorgon, juggler of fire. This man's parents died in a burning house. But Gorgon ran through rings of fire as a tot and escaped. He's been jumping through rings of fire ever since. He'll juggle fire for you now."

Gorgon stepped up, dressed in a red sportscoat, tuxedo, and white tights. In white face his countenance blossomed like an alabaster lily.

He flourished high a number of bowling pins, and laid them on the sidewalk and he lit their ends until they flamed. One, two, three, four, five, he hurtled the flaming pins into the air, a vivid circle of fire he formed with flaming pins.

"Wonderful," Katrina exclaimed.

"Wonderful," Henry exclaimed, applauding wildly, as they'd applauded Boudine.

The man stepped aside with a great bow and next approached a tiny, delicate little woman in white tights.

"Welcome please, Nancy," the ringmaster cried, in vibrating braggadocio, and snapping his whip to good effect, "the greatest little trapeze artist in the world today. Nancy's father died in a telephone line accident. In Wichita, Nancy's mother found work as a seamstress with our troupe, mending the lion tamer's pants. But the high-wire life was for Nancy. She's been with us since 1969 perfecting her art. We're off to L.A. this week. Come see Nancy two weeks from Tuesday at Brooks Hall. She's wonderful, unbelievable," the ringmaster cried, carny to the hilt.

"We will, we will," Katrina exclaimed, for the ringmaster's enthusiasm was infectious.

"I'll buy two tickets," Katrina exclaimed, dipping into her purse. "I'm going to bring my daughter."

"I'll buy two, too," said Henry. "For mine."

"Wonderful, wonderful," the ringmaster cried, pocketing the cash. "My name is Toledo. I come from a long line of Spanish ringmasters. Thank you my lady and my lord, the little people appreciate your support."

"Forward gang," he urged the troupe. "We've much of the city to cover by sundown."

The procession waved feathered caps and bowling pins, batons, swords, and hoops, and black hats, as they bid the two adieu.

"Come to the show and witness these and other amazing feats," the ringmaster cried, vibrato thrilling and hearty even in diminution, a skillful advocate to the last.

Across the street a small cluster of tourists, including Henry's posers, gathered, snapping photos, at this motley, fantastic crew. As the procession moved off the tourists clicked. The *Little People's Circus* invested the afternoon with a charming freshness and variety. The block seemed desolate indeed, though the sweet smell of peonies and begonias from the nearby park nudged their fancies gently, after the troupe had vanished. Had there ever been such a fantastic crew?

The whole little ceremony, such as it was, took a few minutes. Yet the impression of color and motley affability and the wondrous, sparkling humor of the little people impressed her like a dream. Katrina dipped into her pocketbook, half for the purpose of reinforcing the information that she'd received from the ringmaster and fix it in her mind, and in equal part to substantiate the incident.

She pulled the two tickets out. Real it had been; no dream. She had two tickets to the *Little People's Circus* at Brooks Hall.

"Do incidents such as this occur regularly in this city?" Katrina wondered. She felt rather like Alice in Wonderland, in a new kingdom shiny and glistening in the wake of the circus, she was half-ready to believe the rules in the kingdom were more fantastic than the rules in the kingdom that she was accustomed to, she prepared to suspend reason and believe.

"Hardly," Henry replied dryly. "This isn't Disneyland you know, and I never heard of the *Little People's Circus*. Only with you here would this have happened," he joked. "Never would this have happened to me, if I'd been by myself."

They chatted as they walked, quite relaxed with each other.

"So where does your ex-husband live now?" he asked.

"He settled here with Debbie, not too long ago. Did not tell me, up and moved with her, legalized child-stealing, what I call it, though he had a piece of paper saying he could. Debbie writes that she likes it a lot; of course, she misses me."

"And your folks in Topeka?"

"My dad's been dead a number of years. I'll spare you the details. My two sisters and I had it rough, he was an alcoholic. My mother lately turned to the church, for consolations. Away, away, the bird must fly away to see the day," she cried. "Nothing for me back there, I'm afraid. I have a sister modeling in New York, giving that a go, my other sister's in Florida, and runs a flower shop."

"Sounds rough," he sympathized. "Yeah, families. Speaking of which my father had the gall to ring me up a couple months ago, and we met in the Merchant Marine Union hall, us both being members. He clapped me on the back, and shook my hand, as if he'd left the day before, tried to charm the pants off me he did, told me he'd been thinking about his children. It weighed heavy on him, he said. I started reminding him, "Danny's in Phili, man. He's got AIDS. May still be going to bars, picking guys up. He often talks about you, calls you a ghost. You left our mother destitute—with two small kids, and no support.' He's charismatic, and he talks wonderfully. He's got 19th century eyes, and a Herman Melville forehead. He's traveled all over the world, in the Merchant Marines. I kind of admire him. Because he got out. I love him and I hate him both. But I cannot forgive him, not even close yet. Something worth loving is worth fighting for. He got furious, at my fury. Said he'd hoped to find a man, and found a boy, living in the past."

"After 20 years he shows up, wants a meeting?" Katrina exclaimed, indignantly. "That's gall. Families, no wonder they are called nuclear."

"They're a flowerbed and a graveyard both, it's where the bodies are buried," Henry responded, dismissing him with a wave. "It takes money to move. Are you set up okay?"

"A little, from the settlement," replied Katrina. "After they certified I was sane, I had a right. I had hospital bills. But I met a friend at Farley's—the nuthouse—and she gave me, lent me, moving money. I went in there and met one of the sanest, most beautiful people," exclaimed Katrina, and there were tears in her eyes at the thought of her dear friend. "Her name's Cassie O'Shaughnessy. Her family perished in a car accident. She's not really insane—just sad. She lent me."

"An angel," responded Henry. "You have an angel, Katrina. That's good, sailors need their angels to watch over them on their voyages, and you're a sailor, Katrina."

"When she gets her act together she may join me out here," Katrina affirmed. "I hope she does."

How Henry felt about his companion he could hardly express. He felt, in the new morning that comes with new beginnings, spring thrusting out of the soil, and breaking crusts of the old season, and he resolved to ask her out. Her blond river radiance, at times contravened, strove with sturdy determination, rising from the ashes of a bad marriage, or whatever, he could feel her struggling like a baby in its birth throes, in a way, as they walked side by side, her first day on her own, in town.

As for Katrina, she felt his presence positively looming at times, other times laid back and youthful, felt his responses and the beat of her heart when she talked about her family, and despite his occasional scowl, a responsive, queasy stirring. They brushed shoulders occasionally as they walked.

Thus the pair descended the hill, and arrived at the Y, and began phase 2 of their adventure.

The man behind the desk had an ear to the phone, and an eye on the TV, but smiled in a friendly fashion, towards the lady, Henry observed. Freed up after a few moments, he launched into information concerning rates, at their request, noting also information tacked onto the wall. He was a tall man, with a fair complexion, and sandy blond hair. He spoke seriously enough, like he'd done it all before.

"There are three size rooms with three size rates," he smiled, with tight lips, speaking directing to her, after ascertaining she would be the guest/client.

"You have an option of a bath for $20 a month extra, with the larger room," he explained. "You have to pay the Piper cash, no checks please." Not only thorough, but friendly.

Henry asked the man what his interests were. The man replied he was an unemployed actor.

While he showed them a few rooms, Henry established that the lodgings were safe and secure, and mentioned the *Little People's Circus* that had made such an impression. "This town," responded the fellow, with a shake of the head, "where do they come from?"

Having decided on a room, key in hand, they walked together and entered, and shut the door.

"Will you go out with me?" Henry wondered, while she sat, testing her new bedsprings.

A part of him anticipated dazzled evasions, and so on, and he did not mean to rush her, but he was feeling good about her, and was hoping, given his impulsive question, perhaps a conciliatory gesture, a charming, mitigating olive branch, if not a definite answer, under the circumstances.

"I'm tired of being ashamed of what happened to me, you know. I don't feel I should have to spend the rest of my life apologizing to the world about it either, and being ashamed, do you?"

"Of course not," Henry responded, refusing to be put off. "What did happen to you?"

But she had that dazzled, dreamy look again, the look she wore when she spoke about dropping masks, and Henry was confused.

She pointed to a bird, a red cardinal perched on a telephone wire, outside the window, between the gap in the two buildings. "See that bird on a wire?"

"I do," replied Henry, following the arc of her arm, and stopping at the bird.

"Retrieve that bird, take it in hand, and I'll go out with you," she said.

"But it's too high," Henry protested, scandalized. "I don't have the equipment to climb the pole. I'd probably get electrocuted if I did. In any event, any self-respecting bird would fly off if he saw me coming." Henry looked at her if she was serious, she did not appear to be jesting. "What kind of game are you playing, Katrina?" he responded, and scowled.

Katrina's throaty laughter sent a quivering current of electricity down his spine, it was a pleasant laughter full of promise, with a hint of the call of the wild, transported things in life beckoning. But when he turned to her she had that dazzled, dreamy look, she was lost to him, flew into another band of being, far from him, and left him wondering if he were but a jester, in her new room.

He shook this off, and checked over the room, taking command of the situation. He tested the bedsprings with her, bouncing about. She got up, and he scoured the mattress for tears, or bed bugs. He expressed his approval, that though the place looked sparse, and the picture of the Maine winter featuring an obtuse moose was hilarious, the place was in decent shape, considering. He marched down the hall, and found the shower, and found it functional, and the stall tolerably scrubbed, and not ankle deep in dirty water, anyway.

The dresser drawers he plied in and out, lit the gas range. She fluttered about distracted like a butterfly, while these simple tasks he performed for her; in short, playing the man.

What a tumult and tumble of contradictory emotions confronted him as he rode the battered elevator down, fondly cursing the world, the air! On the one hand, she called him a hero, and gave him a goodbye peck on the cheek, and looked on him with hot, bright eyes, and on the other hand was fluid, evasive, when asking for a date. On the one hand, they had achieved a living connection, a real bond, revolving around their mutual parenthood, their daughters, their apparently dire family background, and upbringing, and on the other hand, on a few occasions, their conversation plunged into shadow, and evasions. The more she revealed, the less he understood, or more accurately, the more he wanted to know. Until by the end, by the time he

31

threw her key down, and left the rest to fate, he felt rather in the dark.

The beautiful, haunting girl, whose totem was the cat, with her tattered suitcase, and her big handkerchief, Henry would not see her for two months. He saw his daughter, Daisy Jane on the weekends, and took her to his softball games, and once to Disneyland. The *Little People's Circus* came and went; he did not attend. What if she gave him the cold shoulder there?

After a few weeks, he checked the restaurant, and Donna informed him that she had quit. She had gotten another job, she did not know where. Likewise, she had checked out of the Y. The desk offered no forwarding address. (Or in a quantum world, he did not go to the Y. He let it slide, having no heart for outright rejection. He did not want to be her friend. He wanted her.)

Would he ever meet a person like her again; for one might go a lifetime, he felt, without such luck!

He felt every so often like he had botched his opportunity, and disappointed himself, at love's market, sad to say, and come up short.

After work, he took long walks by the ocean, filling his ears with the roaring waves. "End of land's sadness/end of land's gladness," was that from a poem?

He recalled the two staggering drunks, observing their course from the snack counter, on a collision course with her. Katrina, rather than tame these beasts, infuriated them, because their charges fell like rain as she failed to respond, exciting their malice, and she was blocking their way. The disappointments in his life lay like a concealed weapon, but she revealed the hero in him beneath it.

He walked on, a lonely figure in the fog at nightfall, remembering how she had turned her face to his in the wake of the *Little People's Circus*, a river-blond mermaid, and wondered, "does this happen every day?"

Sally, his girl friend from work, slept above her covers one warm summer night, and her brilliant, white body lay exposed, in the sultry heat, and he regarded her estranged. The achings in the flesh being what they were, he had taken up with her again, but this night something called him, he barely remembered who he was, after a few drinks. As he rose to open the window wider, his heart filled with loathing at his unfinished life, and an image flared outside the window, laughing at him. It was his father. He could see the drunken sailor's face laughing, as he cracked the window open wider with his hand, and the shattered glass tumbled down like diamonds into the street. The Devil. Or perhaps his reflection, caught unawares?

With a surgeon's deliberation he appropriated a towel, amid Sally's concern and fluttering, and wrapped it tightly around his hand, brushing off Sally's hysterics. "I have to follow the dream, otherwise I die," he exclaimed, enigmatically. "Maybe tomorrow I'll quit, and make arrangements to ship out to sea," he declared, his hand pulsing. He felt like a lion with a thorn in his paw, a lion for whom a healing time had come.

"Dude, what happened to your hand?" inquired Bill at work.

"Oh, a little something I picked up in Australia," Henry replied glibly.

"My God, what happened to your hand?" inquired

Sherri at work.

"Oh, a little something I picked up in England," Henry joked.

2
Joseph's Story

"Joseph, are you watching?"

"Joseph," he said.

He leaned forward and touched me lightly.

"I am watching," I said.

His fingers depart, but he stays with me, his presence asserted in the quiet. He sits in the chair he has sat in every night since we came to this place, a box of matches and cigarettes laid out on a small table just within arm's reach. We do not often speak. Elevators somewhere off in the bowels of the building rise and descend, at the threshold of sense, whirring faintly like starry traffic, swishing to the roofs and back. Water gurgles over our heads, and in the darkness gurgles for me. Something to fly on and something to float on have I here in this capsule room. Now he raises his head. Match flares under chin, skull bent licking lips. Hand tanned and stolid, in light of falling dust.

Water, I need water. Perched like an owl in a tree, I hoot the hoot of knowledge. Through these dreary hours. Though my relatives live, most of my relations seem dead. And I am as impartial to my knowledge as is a dead man to his tomb. I feel betrayed, but I am not quite certain. The traitors slip anonymously between our cellular conceptions and had slipped so long before I was born. I have long ago given up the war. The garlands of a seer sink like a stone. I am sorry. To offer myself up as a victim pure and perishable. Like the twisted wheels of the mangled, final machinery. To be banished from the public squares for oblique references. For the look whose only mirror is another's eyes. Alone now with the broken tables of our law, in another world's room I sit. Where I have watched events march like processions as the years pass by.

But I know it takes too long to grow old, and to have earned my wisdom—and it is no content to be young and wise. I know I am too young to be taken seriously.

II

When I was young and small and did not suffer the consequences of my intuition, one day I wanted to be a shadow. While walking down the street enough away from home, I first noticed it. Black and fantastic, it lorded it over me all the way back. To escape the shadow became imperative, and with an instinct that cut to the heart of the matter, I yearned thereafter to become it, and assume the awful shape. That wish vanished abruptly, in this little game, when I observed that dwarf-like shadows with bent, muscled backs belonged to me as surely as did the giants I adored and secretly wished to become. In my eyes now these giants were discredited for consorting with such disappointing companions. It was only later that I observed the gnarly, muscular dwarves nibbling quietly at my heels.

III

Open telephone books collecting dust, where are our friends? His newspapers too, which crumple. There is a radio somewhere, playing country music, soft and low.

Perhaps sounds drifting through ceilings, into our ears below. His glazed eyes, going through a bad stretch. I feel why he has come down here. To gather strength, for revenge. First a divine recuperation—then revenge. His body is dense and stupid, unthinkingly takes up space. Sometimes under a blanket he puts his fingers inside his pants, when he thinks I sleep. This would not be so bad except for Anna. It makes me think of her. He's thinking of her when he does it. I know because I am extra sensitive. Yes, I have gifts. I am laden with gift and curses.

His newspapers are scattered here. We hear the scurry of rat's feet in the dark, every so often. We're having trouble with the toilets. We are mere onlookers now. Where does the light come from? Filters in like dirty linen from window grates, creeps under crevices, or through apertures. Sure we hung things up but they fell down. No stick. Nothing to read but the damn papers because I obviously can't leave here.

Sleep in the nude on warm summer nights, big city working above me. Trucks explode, very far away. For awhile we talked. For a month or so before it became old. I thought we were brothers, that we shared a commonality of sorts, or the certain segments of an identical whole. That we had been pulled into the same arches. Our tracks masterminded to this.

Essence of fires, emanations of water...they are lost on him. And I do not know where to search for these things. This room we have come to, me saying always; I have treaded this ground before; I have said these words before. O most fully delivered horror! This day

I do not see, living by hearsay. This form next to me whom I most love. In this fully compassionate moment. The moonmoths come by night and make us imagine shapes before our yes. We have had very similar dreams in content. That is, the images we have had by night are often shared. Yet we deploy them in our own irreversible fashions. So much so that one understands the meaning of unique forms perhaps. The reason I have come here? It is very simple. But it also recapitulates much that is difficult to understand. I do not understand yet. But, hah! I am so much here...

IV

What blue fish is it that climbs the falls struck by the moon's religious gaze? Like him, I too am moonstruck. Not from without but from within I am struck, as an instrument is struck most fully into tune. There are others, like he beside me, who have been struck by the sun. These sun-struck ones are, in turn, moved to strike whereas we are not. We are struck only. We do not strike except to defend. Even of that I am unsure. For we are at heart indefensible, as we represent the inkling devoid of the shell, the resonance not the blow. My heart beats often like a musical instrument. O sensitive, sensitive. I drink the thing slowly and fully. I move with that grace of fragile things, tenuous as glass. Only the sky can feed me, mouth of clouds, beard of earth. Because I had access to it, because it nursed me and nourished me, because I gave myself up to it in this acme of confidence possible to

41

some spirits, I was permitted entrance into its secrets and privations. I was cloaked, too, in its talents. And because I made myself a mad gift to it, likewise made itself a gift to me, which is often called grace. And they grew jealous of my talents, jealous even of my privations, as children that do not understand but yet feel the ineluctable within their presence, and are moved to anger at one who lives there. In my capacity to feel what they could only see, I was termed outcast; in my plenitude of vision where they could only sleep, I was termed dreamer. But who stole their capacity to receive these favored signals? From where stemmed their inability to be buoyed up by other than their own inventions? Surely something had been lost, withered, whether deserted or forsaken, for what possible causes? He sitting next to me snores quietly, dreams mayhaps he is leading a demonstration, in our nest.

They did not understand my extravagances, which was the extravagance of a force exerted through me; I have powers; neither could they accept the sights which I reported, for how could they when their own eyes, unbelieving, stamped upon them their abysmal schemes. Dreaming on ash heaps, they called it, or some such. But unconvinced they did me injury nevertheless, due to they felt I was beyond them.

V

The scythe of the hours passing. The tawdry blankets on the rickety chairs. We could break out, and go hiking in the mountains. We have walked woodsy trails, with hawks circling over our heads, and stags rackety in the underbrush, a glimpse of ewes among the brake. My heart rate has been rebuffed by the age I live in. They with the masks, thinly tied, are guilty. When I had my fingers spread where their eyes trailed, they swore to it once and for all. I, innocent of harm, proctored the sky. Calyxes of images fell homeward. Watchman, I. All in the meaning of a man. Cross the Ariel yard birds over whiffs of salt-breeze, and sailboats in the distance. Tacking in the breeze. Who understood the tragic then?

They seized me. Cremated me in their minds with fires from filthy sex acts. My robes they tore from my back in a frenzy of nails. My many colored coat ripped from my back. Livid apostasies which appeased no one 'til brought home to flesh. My father's sons. Brandishing their terrible weapons of manhood thus pressed against me. The masses opening irregular sores which never healed. He beside me exempt and yet inclusive. For the injuries done to others make small the injuries done to me.

Do rabbits dream of ditches as they couple? But we are not rabbits. Stars, even, convey our fancy. All so large makes yet the largest thing seem small, breeding such proportions in our mind. The musty cubicles, our sad retreat, disdain contempt. Only the stars do not. H. beside me rarely dreams really, but periodically confuses the daytime-met images in night. Where acts only follow act though, devoid of clear surroundings, there they scourge the mirrors. He never dreams really, for are his eyes fully developed enough to close? I, who feel contempt, which is the great riser that throws fear up to the stars, am contrariwise blessed with the temptation to love. Fragrant air, versus rains of dust. My life sees, though admittedly in vague, and rapidly falsifying way. The warm eye, the cold eye, holds me in stead. For the quality of the vigil is known too by its plight. Through the dark of the night of my vigil here, with the figure dense beside me, I am held in stead.

VI

Bandy about all the tongues you have been taught. The miseries continue. Charge with energies, life excavates its secrets. There are the young-at-heart, growing into new experiences. There are the grand operas. Swinging on a rusty gate. We crouched beside a large wooden cave before dawn. The sun rose awesomely in the east. What animals gathered there, blinking their eyes? The process is committed to the day, but the idea to the night. Holes of men with plant-like tendencies were stoppered up, to survive. Thus the energies for religions. The memories stayed like a bone in our throat, causing us to gag upon the galaxies. Sprinkle of stars representing such nausea across the sky. Ho ho ho. Grasp the curtain which wants to hide from itself by being used. For your own eyes sake, clasp. Bodies whose flesh is dark and thick, or translucent as a slight possibility. Anna said to me; hold steady in the moonlight. For in the dark is constantly reprieved the soul of man. My excursions were her delight. Now what wan light falls down on the mattress where she once lay? She could rough it with the best of them, and make breakfast in the morning. From the room I can hear the whine of generators, undiminishing. To have looked into the spaces of the mouth where the chewing occurs, there's the rub. Whether with pain as fully conscious, or with cares. He is not man, though, if he does not respond. Idle in this room, yet rushes my capacity to delve. H. stood knee-deep in horror only once removed. For this I respect him fully, and yet, are my terms precise? The print on his radical newspapers fade. He eats intelligently as he grows healthier once again. He will be thinking of leaving soon. It makes me want to talk with him, but I know it is useless to try. We wrapped up in blankets cast two small shadows on the floor. The rings around the room and our eyes betray our problems. Come home to me now all resources!

VII

The burning in my fingertips. Meshed with my eyes walking around the room on a shaft of light. If the universe were a fully gray matter, it would have collapsed by now due to its lack of sinew. I could imagine God, not cold, slender and weary, after having turned away from himself to perform feats which, titanic and disruptive, are yet strangely final. The ache of his head and his artist's hands. Sensitive to pain and the other obscure entropies, ever returning and dumb. If he could control, then creation would be a play. But this is not, it is he who turns away, shell-shocked and weary. He was just a young man, a lover of wild life. His original perceptions were full of hope. When was it that he first came up against his materials? How was it that his dreamed magnificence's were caught looking so fully at themselves? This room even now is slowly sinking in the bedrock of his fancies. What a high pitch of intensity he had prepared himself for. But lo, the materials were his undoing. For such weights it was clear he was not ready. Stubborn, stolid, intransigent. Inflexible, unmanageable. He was a child to think in terms of shapes, but the only thing he knew were visions! Such an innocent. Then to lie back perhaps, in a bed the size of sky. Never thinking, what will you do when your body ends? The logic of the far-off residing in his need to turn away from himself, and test his dreams on lumps of clay.

In the dark of the primeval night, his eyes which moved through rock, were beaming. He lifted himself upon an elbow where he lay floating in mid-chasm or dis-illusion, neither fulfilled nor yet disinterested, half imparted into stone, half-reserved, from which attitude we make our dreams. And the wishing well is the size of the universe, with no bottom but our receding eye, light speed. Telescoping such proportions to keep us sane.

VIII

Rope hangs from the ceiling casting a shadow on the wall. Sing on, lambs! Softly playing country music from an apartment above.

The sky is merely a suggestive shape, but who has

explored the mind which makes it infinite? My friend sits in the corner, and regroups, deep in sleep. But each object, regarded properly, becomes a trinket. And life itself an instrument for even greater occasions than habitually realized. But this comes to me through dreams! Dreams are the bond between me and the riddle of creation. Did I dream this, or did someone say this? Without them, lovelorn and weary, where are we? O the augury of man, couched in a smattering of dust? The crust of insubstantial omens our meal, cause we're all gonna die. And yet the individual, out of the hole from which he came, drinks, and it is good. Of two creatures, I discern; the drinker and the mover, the artist and the builder. Each flows into the other, in degrees. Countless issues rising and falling, repeatedly endlessly anew, by a process devoid of contemplation. Sibilant corn under a harvest moon. Lurid ardors that inspire strange directions. How far we drifted from the source. Where fingertips unfurl in a mirage communication. H.'s body heaves itself regularly like a small machine. Down from the seat to the cot my fiery friend has sunk. Personality, such a recent and hazardous development, of little staying power? The majority of this plane's fingertips not yet graced with fingerprints?

For those with minuscule memory of need and grand vision, sweep on. Though it be an ocean, farewell! But know this place I am in is not coincidental, and the watchman affirms his vigil. Each of us has our part to play.

IX

The darling, cuddly ball of fur, my first cat Muffy.
Two soft figures in the backseat sat, their Mom driving
us home from school maybe, remember the car, a light
Chevy sedan, two sisters, Janice and Doris, Doris told
me her cat had baby kittens, would I want one? Did not
dare to ask my mother and father, likely as not they'd say
"No." A black and white patched bundle of energy and
determination during the day, gentle and comforting at
night. The mewling, meowing kitten. The stalwart adult.
Would sleep with me in bed. Every so often nuzzle the
blanket so ardently, I'd throw him off. Did he take me for
his mate?

Years of the yellow bus that took me to school, my
sister with her pink socks and all, my younger brother
learning to ride his bike. On a golden afternoon, after
school, playing baseball with the kids in the 'hood.
George, though thin and not nearly as tall as the Gatto
brothers, always picked first, he could blast home runs
over the fence. There was Billy, Tommy, from up the
street, Jack from the other side of the development,
who'd ask me "how they hangin?" Bruce, who became a
dentist, and Jeff, who became an accountant, and Pat who
became a cop. Pat could be scary.

All together on a breezy spring day, in yesteryear
forever, small figures dodging the shadows, (shadow
puppets) laughing and playing in the sun, until the sky
darkened, and we got called in for supper by our moms. I
remember, I remember.

X

A lamp is fixed. I have endeavored to twist a lightbulb in a significant way. So, the soil of our lives. A little water, perhaps one begins to fructify, to grow.

As for me, I find some days I eschew the light. It was apparent to me that it was squashing any impulse that one might have to disown the public impulses, that one is heir to. For example, one could walk down the street and if you looked at everything in a certain light, it was imminently understandable. If you looked at things only in the proper light, it was very clear. So then I would think, tell me you strollers, what exactly is the state of your world on this very clear morning under your certain light? Drug store, clothing store, bakery. Then I would imagine turning, in mid-answer the beams by which they gathered their perceptions into things unknown, altering reality, deranged. Calmnesses would be transposed into centers of meaningless activity, networks into vast webs gone spatially awry. The mountains and heavy matrices would become nets glistening with human blood, and systems transformed into disposal units. All symbols would become echoes out of a dark cave which no one understands. All reasons and alertnesses would fall before indefinable onslaughts of sensation. In this way I imagined undermining the very systems which were hoisted above the sun, and permitted no one a feasible expression of their basically legitimate experience here. How I survived those years, walking in the light of profound derangement, is beyond me. Of course my feelings were shot, but this seemed only normal. Hell could have come and gone without me being awakened by my slumber. And this is the slumber of the universe! Now, after the trauma, disabilities, the still-caked blood, and after the appraisal delivered too harshly to my eyes, after the gnashing of lips and the pain, after the railing which sapped me of my strength, like a lover I walked into the profound gaze of the thoughtful night. Youth plays around with derangement, to separate the wheat from the chaff, mayhaps, and seems so ultimate and daring at the time.

I demolished much, but even courage was not involved. No, it was simply a matter of taste! I could not breathe for lack of air in that treadmill of dreams, willingnesses, where beings slumber vertically, so I simply took my leave. O, and do not think to thicken me, pity me, you bluebeards out there watching. I much prefer my private fantasies to your public ones.

You, stuck in odors, could never have been my teachers. Where you have been for 40 years I have been through in a minute, and lifted my hand, cavalierly bored. How all your lies to hold me fall on their vacant face. And I have been freed finally to experience sweet consciousness, in the freedom-loving night...

XI

What a laugh? I, free? A slight breeze ripples through this room like an event. H. has studiously smoked his last pack of cigarettes today, and seems at a loss for something to do. How long has it been since I have seen a street? His old newspapers give off a smell something like urine, or the odor of rotting wood. These were his vision, his glory, and his fame. Now committed to this irrevocable dust. Ah, the thunder in my head, it is decreasing. All storms you know, were thrown across the sky, and measure out our fury. But here in this room surrenders stalk so easy. Let it be a test then. As to how soon a soul intrinsically sky-born sinks down to the size of a room which covers him over.

Now, upon the wall, the fervent shadow of a man raises his fingers to the stars. And in the dark arm-chair his counterpart can also be seen laughing, bitterly amused...

XII

Anna has come back! Though the day breaks lie a thousand storm-troopers, she has come back. I know I do not deserve it. My suffering has never allowed me sufficient compensation up 'til now. Why should this begin here?

Anna has come back. Like the spring breeze thither returning. Across the anthers and meridians. On a silent beam of hope. Where the anguish of hands turns huge in contemplation. Where shadows throw reality out of kilter. Where objects turn one numb and press one under. We're on the run from the law. Where the air bathed in blue hunger gnaws one's vitals. When the skim of wind seems gale-force.

Anna has come back. Now fear images go under. I will

wipe you off my wall. Off the face of those things where you have been crawling, with very dirty feet. Brief and lonely but a minute here, Anna has returned.

You whose eyes are like keys as deep as truths
You whose body is a thousand large sensations
You whose winds awash the air with plaintive ardors
You whose mind awakens stirring breaths
You who have been at the center of the matrix

Yes.

You who bring the apple in its season
You whose colors replace morality
You whose capacities are cups for larger things
You whose meditations float whole continents
You whose cordage is backbone of the starts.

Now everything has altered. Appearance itself is quite symbolic. And I am growing enamored with the possible large consequences in my position. Oh, H. in the creaking chair through the long and limping night. You too must be feeling my thoughts. How wide the moat, the flesh, the time? Where were we in the world's eyes all this while? Displaced in some strange fashion that is beyond me and my formative powers. Now no more the loneliness, and the night without personal interest. No more the empty glasses, though filled with eyes. Anna has returned.

XIII

Kiss her on the neck. Freedom thoughts come. Kiss her on the mouth. Warmth sensations come.

The sunlight falls on crusts of plaster. We were walking, then, walking. Saw the heavy women with their Japanese babies. The purveyors of strange events. All things revolving through her hair. We were free, then, free. The winds, trees, dawns were brought home to strange eyes under a magnificent day, which glowed through like a fiery parcel. What receded and was never heard from again? What calms under stars, from within the inner reaches, reaching up, did we experience? What crowds of sensations on the way to the Statue of Liberty! How crazy dense and heavy the traffic, how sullen the multitudes. How green the face of the great lady, glimpsed from the spiral stair, looming above us while we climbed. There, hands filling pocket, or mouth turned groping, one illumination beset me. With the children yelling from the windows, with the fire-engines screaming, and careening. Amidst the matrix of hours, buildings, miles trodden. This eternal moment, never repeating, stretching out in its wonderful infinity of sadness, a symphony here and gone. Within my pounding head as well, one other gaining entrance. Anna has come back.

It was a matter of communion, beds, speech, the rising and falling of events which constitute our life. It was a matter of my swollen solitude. She knew me in my prime! I had a style which was bequeathed to me by the gods themselves. This all pinpointed towards her

53

eye, her affections. I was ready for the extraordinary and conveyed to her the impression I could love it. No secretness of purpose was beyond me, no subtleness lost to my perception. I satisfied her need for the ineffable, which she became convinced I was in touch with. Sole question, when would the breakthrough come? Vanity of vanity, saith the preacher.

Finding refuge in her arms, or upon her woefully soft and heaving breast, I vowed to give up the search. I realized I probably could get no closer. She was a dancer. She with her longings, and otherworldly expressions, with her chases, and her reveries in the shadows, where she drew resource beyond my ken, she was Other, clearly a gift. She felt the pull of the universe on her body, within her bootsy body. Oh, exquisite tremors! There she strove to keep it, at the center of forces beyond me. What a small body! Such compression that astounds one, like a miniature star! Ah, under the sky full of passion, where images are breathes of flight, all things occur simultaneously. Do not even ask me! And yet, though firmly and deeply embedded, her eyes would gaze from her face with such serene (seraphic) clarity to make me wince! She sensed it all, and extraordinary wonder and terror, operated on it!

XIV

The black triangular mass of fur. Which it always comes down to, from before when I was born. To long after.

I will give you a hint about my problem. I take nothing for granted. It is all here, granted, but I cannot take it. Always thinking as if, as if. What precisely was in my mind to make such things come to pass? You see the, as if? Summer turns to fall, and me trying to remember what it was I had in mind.

XV

Perhaps we could go on as three. Or will Anna ride off into the sunset with H.? We turned our eyes to each other then, asking.

H. is now suddenly teeming with life. His legs shake up the place, which he feels has been transformed into an auditorium. His arms are full of memorable, or reproducible gestures. Have I told you that she loves him? Anna has come to sit with us, and the dramas build. She loves him for the fact that he is not bottomless. A brief but startling aura of electricity surrounds Anna when she sleeps. My gifts are receptive. These capacities are like a wooden board where I moaning, climb up, and get nailed to. How easily it would be to survive simply! Real life which demands nothing but an operational definition, unquestionable, devoid of real knowledge. All the jewels in the seas, sky, nights miscellaneous phenomenon, on a backlit stage in the background. I suspect the much-vaunted integrity of our systems are being a fiercely dissolving mist to expire in. All the boats, offices, relations, not sufficient to keep us floating. Though ignorance, here, is of certain value.

How charming H. is in his near sightedness. Learn to be superficial, an artist cried, near death. He is more photogenic than I. And all of us desire those comforting images to protect us against the nine desolations, frightening unease. We're here on borrowed time, on a short term lease. This is the part of our weakness we carry through years, lovers, sure as breath.

XVI

I remember once woods like a cathedral. Wafting breezes, through willowy trees, all the earth seeming open, and out-gushing. From out of the ground tremendous things arose. The green of hills arched into shapes that seemed religious. Birds graced the rolling meadows. God seemed to shine with nature's bounty, in the sun.

There, comfortable in the deep rhythms, I was loathe to judge. Everything flowed through, like an inevitable act. Some huge fatality, not odious, came over me there. There, fully sane, and full, amid the flowers, rolling streams, the world seemed to tremble in all its strength and frailty, amid the sky and shadow which gives stir onto our blood, amid the setting sun and the coming twilight, with its tender mysteries, that held danger and menace in abeyance, from a bounty of good. Nights young, and full of hope, the organ of the sea storm, the white cloud that made me still. Who was I to speak?

What incredible pieties without hypocrisies! We build the machinery to try and protect ourselves, and it often proves to be the horrible mouth we were trying to protect ourselves from. And what is humanity once denuded of the anesthesia inherent in the tragic process, where, reaching, responding within, we reach beyond ourselves, get into a greater zone, reunited in a broader harmony. Where we, so pale, have no blood to redeem it? The big sleep and redemption all fled!

Oh Joseph, you are finely caught. You no more possess the magic to turn about. Sing,

> *buildings with a thousand windows*
> *every window filled with light,*
> *see nothing, nothing is what's dreamed*
> *as night rolls into stricken night.*

Anna with the long hair, dark, reclines besides your foot. H. is reading his newspapers again.

XVII

H. is a revolutionary. Listen, here is what he has to say.

There can be no mediation. History has shown us that! We, born into a grip of evil unparalleled in its subtlety, must clearly fight. Otherwise we are theirs, and serve to propagate the very perverseness which we oppose.

If there were easier ways then we would take them. But what they have done to us, the way in which they make people live, then convince them that it is natural, the distances that they have put between our heads and our hearts, is of such a magnitude that only combat in the face of it is feasible, or natural...

Then.

The people, them I dearly love. It is for my sake as well as theirs I do this. I want to live on this planet before it expires, and for the children I may have also. A reevaluation of our values is in order, the wishes of its inhabitants be accessed to reinvigorate the horizons, repopulate its body...

And finally...

We live in the heart of the corruption, victims of greed by our leaders. At this time, the many have been hoodwinked, or duped into their service, but this will not always be so. So much injustice afoot will gradually be recognized. The forces which bend the backs of us all will gradually be named...

There! You see how unapproachable he is! Perceptions as lucid as icicles! Yet certainly he cannot be faulted. Yet he continually astounds me with his lack of a darker, more inner compartment which I may appeal to. Ah, my brethren out there as victims of the natural phenomena, blood gushing from your ear, or stretched out upon the pavement, sleeping. And here one sits who has been crushed repeatedly, by forces larger and deeper than even he suspects.

He will never learn entirely though, for he is still too much the thing he is fighting. He is still too much the weapon, is mind too much targeted. And where he steps will he ever fully understand, too clearly bound for the place he is bound for? How may I help him? His manner of breathing, so pointed, depends on the formation he attacks. He, in reaction, has become an ingrained aspect of that which he would rend through. His strength summoned from the enormity of the dislocation, which he draws from.

What does he know of lives lived for intimations beyond reason? What may he grasp of the network of stars and bone to which our hearts are linked? Or the faces, which, as phantoms, cross and confound the memory? Oh, so straight forward as marching feet he will hew, and direct his energies. Energies, fierce longings, bright powers, with which we arch our soul into their grandeurs.

Remember them H., that they were not intended for total straightness, so as to cast no shadow reverberating, the universe is also curved. You as at your yoke, you become the thing you dislike, I see you grow old with unreality.

Anna, yes, she is here, but do not be deceived. It is a dead hand you choose, when you read so heavily your paper.

XVIII

Sounds through the four walls. The bing of water dripping. Odors of bodies faint in the night-hush.

There, the triangular mass of fur. That it comes down to. From before when I was born. To long after.

Her arm thrown over her head, relaxed. Her slightly announced tongue.

Her body beautifully white, like a new flower. Her mane of hair, dark. Her movements on a gentle sea.

We have had moments on a gentle sea. Yes! There, where the egg bequeathed to the vacuum makes a move. All authored in her organs. We entrancing like before us. Amidst operations suitably shaped.

Oh, Anna. I love to come into contact with your nervous system. So warm, the feeling. Touch me, touch me, touch me! You are my immediate sensation. You are my soft chain to the eternal.

My bowels churn... (Or, Amen)

XIX

Anna breathes and the vicinity comes alive. Her body, I know, is a powerhouse. Her mind is a way-station of fluid, streaming sensation. Her dreams awaken me to emotions I have feared. Her sleeps permit me to think kindly of the night, and the universal burdens.

Her business here is to remember us to ourselves.

H. is eating ravenously. He alternately struts and pouts across the room. All the constraints, frenzies, generosities, are equally remote. One has only to relax; breathe like a child, beard like a man. For whom if not for us were these actions wished for? For whom if not for us dreams palpable, and capable of love? What spirits in world's house wait by door, and seek each other out for restless couple? What phantoms, as I breathe here whole, have stretched themselves out across the galaxies? Ah, words so quick and harmless. You fly up and knock yourself against the ceiling, where shadows spread a wing, and vanish into dust. Surely our fate is to be verbs, or active qualities, in a yearning passage beyond our grasp? A pervasive but perhaps cheaply mystical affair, sponsored by poets? Or a séance in the dark? Participants in an extravagant enterprise. Where ventures turn in the grip of a holy thumb, perhaps bleeding, or are exhibited as charms to ward off what unknowns?

Anna, here is what I have written. It is a poem to the race.

> *the eye is to the sky*
> *what the prick is to the opening*
> *as the eye is a lodger and the sky is its home*
> *so the prick to the aperture*
> *and as man's need for dominance of female parts*
> > *brought about a family structure*
> *so need for dominance of the expanse*
> > *brought about a theory of God.*
> *Both served to permit access to holy territory.*

There, I am quieted. Our fingertips, oh balm of extension, are forever joined. Let sleep and the night of balm come!

XX

She, slim as snakes, has crawled away. Trees bend down in community. Flower stalks berate themselves before the sun. Unnaturalness is rampant. Now no more locked up.

Off she goes, on a weekend trip with H., my shadow twin.

Anna loves to touch bottom. Though a pioneer,

61

in serious times truly it is good to feel secured. Eyes, hair, lips. The connections no more than intuitions, feverishly thought out. The books in cartons, filled with commitments, visions, appraisal, recede. The works of the masters are on paper. Our life transgresses, in real time. Here in the night full of solitude, through the bodies, feelings, organs, our life transpires, slightly felt, amidst the turning of the stars.

We keep this to ourselves as long as possible.

XXI

Daylight of our works! Stones are heaped in the city one upon the other, as if it were planned that way. Indeed! Installed lights enable us to see the road in the dark. Our inventions sway over the totality. Panoramas leap to view, apparently conquered.

But what are men in this year? Numbers in the phase of an equation, being worked out. Ciphers in the ledger in a scrawl more illegible as history progresses? Oh hungers whose appetites are swollen, under the shadow of giant sunspots and melting icecaps! Oh science and visibility you brought us security to a degree, and humanity has been entirely grateful. Your increments had us turn our back on eternity and study things which gave us pride. Your ingenuities made us lust for ingenuity in small places, until we were tangled in magnitudes beneath our dreams. Your seriousness made us respect you, and we grew grave! Your joy, to disrobe only, and when the object of your regard, blushing, undergoes your scrutiny, it must leave, pale and trembling like a ghost.

Oh science and all the stranded similes! You, beautiful austere, to have had such heartless children as police forces, secret files, deadly machines. Your strains of great music, that play to our mind. Your disguising consolations, in the face of ineffable losses, a teetering see-saw. Your bastions between men's dreams and situations. Or am I the irrelevant one, behind the times?

To your muscular arms, oh white one, with which you have untangled the earth, and set our house in order. To your ravaging countenance behind your face full of facts. Will there be compromise, settlement? I salute you! To your emptiness, ever as ultimate, but more cruel.

XXII

Dreamers and movers, thinkers and builders.

Movers move to get things done, confident in the whirl, never turning their heads. Fueled by the heat of a million thriving suns, completing and interpenetrating their circuits, in the grip of a public millennium. Creators of spectacles; whose movement is the primal quality of nature; where deed is the absolute form of definition. These press home across the earth.

Builders. Objects are for removing. They will storm the throne room. Their certainty invades all places.

Their short-term visions imbued with forces tremendously old, and popularly received. Their life spans hurled into vital paths, that may perchance, light the way for many to follow. Edging by degrees, on occasion, into the dreamers and thinkers.

Inklings of intenser harmonies, and all the hazards by which life, subtly, devised a foothold. The clear note of the hill in their ear, formed fully by shape, into wavelength, and apprehended as music. The earth in all its possibilities purely and totally received. The stars hung clear in majesty. Auras and images are of import, for shorthand for the compressed historical process, reverberating their presence through time. In image, may be destiny.

They, the generations of the world's unconscious, generated in order to monitor its directions. The transmitters of the race, along a longer wavelength.

Machine souls, I see you have become weapons. Yes, and all visions merely targets. Across the night of stars, huge masses and migrations have taken place.

Souls and spirits, through the sound of far off laughter and terminologies, you disappeared as through a wreathe of smoke. Green tables now no more speak to us where we once laid down our bodies. The damage done!

I admire Alexander Graham Bell. Bearded Scot via Canada, new to America, dedicated to helping deaf people, students, lead a positive, normal life, in mainstream society. Not hidden away in shame, in a slovenly, decrepit institutional setting, with meager life expectancies. Short shrift!

Began teaching in Boston, and met a formidable young lady, a student, and slowly fell in love. Her wealthy father took an interest in the handsome, eccentric teacher, and his vague notion of a telephone.

Spends years sweating it out, in a tiny shop, with his assistant Watson, tinkering with diaphragms, and dials, and currents, while horse-drawn wagons went by outside, and though Edison also competed to build the device, Bell got their first and won the patent. After suffering a nervous breakdown!

Bell summons up vision in his head first, and builds his dream. The Bell company would successfully defend his patent to over 600 challenges over the years, including from Thomas Edison and Eliza Gray, backed by big money.

Later, forms a league of bright young men, to work on a flying machine, and competes with the Wright brothers, in various flying endeavors.

Also builds a crude metal detector, a hydrofoil, and made important contributions in aeronautics. Never wavered from his commitment to helping the deaf go mainstream, in a heedless society, that had better things to do.

I admire Albert Einstein…

XXIII

Memorial Day weekend, a great way to kick off the summer. Anna and H. go on a road trip, engine humming, up state, into the open.

Yada Yada. So it goes. They looked around, hobnobbed in antique stores, looking for special stuff, Anna's got special tastes (needs), and took a bungalow for a month.

Hunters with guns had taken a room next door, they

found out later. They would hear the thump of hunting boots and every so often gunshots not far away.

Anna did some nude modeling for an artist colony up there. There was also a fat farm up there. She made friends with a few residents there for the month, at a local café.

H., on the other hand, made acquaintances with the hunters. "Not bad guys," he assured me, though shooting little birds is—well—a little retro…

H. hung out with them at the local bar in the evenings, often as not.

Apparently, they had had a big fight over Anna's modeling choices. Also, over her choice of new friends.

"Gee, Anna, they're fat. You're so beautiful, thin and lissome."

"Gee, Anna, baring your body to total strangers…"

XXIV

I admire Albert Einstein. A cultural icon, no doubt.

Revolutionized our (the educated world) perspective on space, time, gravity, electromagnetism.

Doesn't get more real than that, what say?

But Einstein stressed, in his nature, how creative thinking and imagination is more important than the perceived system of things.

"Imagination is more important than knowledge," he'd say.

A serious violin player. Played in a chamber quartet for years, with the likes of Max Planck and Irwin

Schrodinger.

Sitting there in his little patent office in Berne, Switzerland, across from the railway station, and myriad clocks.

A leading Swiss industry making clocks. Brands like Lange, Piguet, Ball, Baume Mercier, Breguet, Breitling, Cartier, Omega, Rolex.

Would he have devised his theory of relativity but that he was surrounded by clocks?

—The German school system rejected him, called him "slow." It did not help perhaps that his views and approaches to problem solving did not always coincide with Herr Professor, his inflexible (rigid) teachers, their authority questioned, perhaps they shut him down, lost interest.

Einstein was basically starving in Germany when he landed a job at the patent office via a connection, a recommendation from a friend's father. Only later did he complete his PhD.

But for that friend's father...

XXV

I'm about endeavoring to trace the structures of reality. The dreamer and the doer, the thinker and the builder. The sweet spot in between.

A mother passes, pushing her baby carriage, the baby sings "gag a goo goo, oh oh oh..."

What does it all signify, being here? The birds in the trees do not ask questions, they sing.

An ornithologist would say, naturally they are hardwired to do what they do. Humans apparently have software, mutable and evolving.

—I'm not so sure. Every so often I have the great notion that birds have been here before, and have chosen their incarnation, that birds are an advanced incarnation, more progressive than ours.

Perhaps they choose to eschew the technological trappings, the modern confusions, and opt for a radical simplicity. Silly? They fly. They sing.

Imagine men who find it thrilling to shoot birds. Sons of bitches.

A bird flew up to me, and hunted and pecked a few inches from my foot, relaxed. There are agents here beyond our ken, bank on it.

Three burly men walk by, the chickadee flies off, a minute later it's back, walking under my foot.

Many of the images are pieces retrieved barely from a dream.

Barely, barely.

Dreams are the connection between me and the riddle of creation.

Suddenly the world is a very cool place, in a park, birds singing in the trees. "Beautiful eyes," the mother coos, sitting on a bench with her friend, cooing over her baby, way-stations of fluid, streaming sensation, a million year young architecture.

XXVI

Ghost are ancient as their griefs. They bemoan, always, the thing that's done. It is not their fault! As if returning to the scene of a crime, tremendous in magnitude, they flood the cellars and attics of the world, sit in flesh of Me.

And the weapons flash out through the long twilight continuously, and imbue the nighttime full of death.

Anna said;

Joseph, I love your darkness, your mystery, your brooding in your nights full of solitude. But I too am seed. Long time the drop, stalk searching tentatively for ground. Finally brought home to you after such long passage.

Then;

It doesn't matter that I see. He is pure light of which we never grow tired.

Then;

Do not go too far away, Joseph. You are a shade upon the world's back,
fully conscious through your days. The breeze, leaves, trees, in
all their turning will never leave you. But the hurt, Joseph, which they do
not even feel, being creature, is fit only for God. Bearable only
by God, and not for men has this pain been kneaded into form.

Now the last collective, delicate noises of our parting fill the room. When I close my eyes the light tells me I am still here.

I am a spirit. I was meant to celebrate. Anna! On the strongest and loneliest back I have made my way, full of strange, incomplete ideas. Our gurgling so impressed me though that I have paid many nights over in the memory.

Processes like smoke were seen to rise and curl away, and I did not believe in them. Whiffs of deeds were far more basic than the deeds themselves. This was seen from the misery and clockwork of our bodies, which I portioned holy. Our lady of the Flowers! With the earth and all its trouble in our hands, though we sometimes asked, where have all the people gone?

The theater of the world heaves a sigh! Our appreciations reach their climaxes at our endings. The whir of tape decks through the brains and years. Our own unreeling episodes. Cast in the networks of such soul and skin.

All the fierce harmonies have gone by. But Anna;

> *when you roll into me in the middle of the night*
> *we're like two creatures of the sea*
> *in calm waters, lapping up the dark*
> *grazing mouth to mouth*
>
> *and in my ears*
> *is the sound of the sea*
> *as the sea rolls over shore*

so you roll over me.

and in my mouth
is the taste of the sea
as I do cover you
and you do cover me

and in my eyes
is the sight of the sea
puling, ever-pulling
silently.

You see that I understand, don't you?

XXVII

Full moons over vacant lots. The barrenness of diffuse events, perpetrated often. The languor and violence which captions a sky without meaning.

Across the world fireplaces keep us warm. Grunts in flesh jackets. Legs opening and closing across the universe.

Our skin is the motto of our soul. Our soul is the value of our skin. How stupidly simple!

Breathe in, breathe out, cripple or slave, woman with child, men without love.

Breathe in, breathe out, drunkards, prisoners pacing in forsaken cells, thieves, knaves of the lowest variety, birds without plumage.

Breathe in, breathe out, fools, poets, lovers.

Breathe in, breathe out, wretchedness of continents, animals washed ashore in the dark, a bone caught in the throat. President of Anguish, riffing on the estate.

Breathe in, breathe out, men without mercy, men in authority.

Breathe in, breathe out, beauties of light and dark, the courage of every living thing.

When I looked out over the world, with my deepset eyes, I became dizzy. For out of it energies it had generated strife.

Deep in the well, where the starlight comes up from within, I saw its face. Deep in the eye, where sight first begins to emerge, I saw the thing that scares me.

Most people are mirrors reflecting the other, but poets are mirrors reflecting the stars.

The universe bestows the stars, galaxies, moons on our faces like kisses in the foreplay of love. But its need is to live on through us. The need is to carry itself on. And our intimations, which are its child through us, is what makes such kisses of light so impassioned.

Watch occasionally, as passion leaps up into beauty. It is our darkness giving birth.

And do not laugh too hard. You will give yourself away. Wear occasionally a coat. But do not mask your needs. The light fills up your eyes, oh beautiful one! But who will speak for the world's wavering millions?

You try to keep it in. You have to let it out. You lie upon the bed. Or work diligently. You find yourself alone. You swiftly locked it up. But it made things passable.

You found a little love. Your friendships make you

weep. You have close ties with your family. After all they brought you up. It's not a minor thing.

You've finally found a heart. You know that this is it. It only happens once. It's good beyond belief. Why did you split so soon?

The ages pile up. You see that things would rather cry. It doesn't make you mad. It carries though some weight. It makes you want to think…but wherefore dost thou ask?

XXVIII

Slow movements behind the quickness of forms. Deep purposes hidden in our eyes. The always beating pulse regardless of ears.

Our lives, a black hair turning to white against a black background. In other ears, the sound of a song. The organs picking up.

(Now all shadows enter in. Our lives are being lived for mystical reasons, happening rarely. Souls and spirits! Come to bear on my own skin.)

Like a bee sipping a flower, I have knelt at life. Ha! The earth is stained with the blood-soaked rags of the millions! It, streaked with music, bleeds unpleasantly at all hours. Forms crumble every which way. However, morning, sweet morning arrives, and their influence departs, vapid as mist.

But we, if I remember have been known to carry our ardors into darkness. Yes! And perhaps though in the flurry of occurrence, the sheer quantities of squalor will lay us low, there are other weights and other doings. Our flesh is capable of other lives! Begone with theories! I long to hold this world together with my personality, like every newborn babe.

It is all here. The black triangular mass of fur. Which it often comes down to. From before birth. To long after. I always thinking, as if, as if. What was in my mind to make such things come to pass? You see the, as if? Snow begins to fall, rain comes down in a vale, and me trying impossibly to remember, what it was I had in mind.

XXIX

There was Michelle, la belle jeune fille, slender, elusive, bubbly among friends, who seemed to be turning sideways at every opportunity among friends, bashful, posing, could never figure her enigmatic style, anyway not sufficient.

There was Gail, beautiful in an eastern way, like Cleopatra or Esther, dignified, reserved, with a sonorous voice, every so often a light touch on the shoulder, we would go out under the stars, and run the college track around midnight, anyway not sufficient.

There was Diane, fulsome, magnetic, who would stand in the room by my door, after locking it, eyes full of promise, sparkling, bosom heaving, ready for action, anyway not sufficient.

Anna would not come until later, each of us caught in the moment, at the moment, the right moment, the one that fit like a glove, Anna.

XXX

Up from below, breaking the surface, the roll call of early deaths, Jimi Hendrix, Jim Morrison, Janis Joplin, Kurt Cobain, Amy Winehouse, members of the 27 club. Like scouts on the mountain they envisioned what later many would feel and live through. Perhaps they saw the cavalry coming, but a cavalry good or bad? Perhaps they viewed the Indians on their way, but the Indians good or bad? Depends in part on whose ox is being gored.

The House of Propriety versus the House of Mystery. The first values the consumer, the producers, the functioning organisms in a larger hive. The second values soulfulness, aura, aspiration, regardless of status, *un petite peu.*

Rimbaud died young, Van Gogh died young, de Nerval, Hart Crane, Emily Dickinson, all in the league of extraordinary, valiant scouts, who tracked, explored, immense journeys, within the world, within the self, while the House of Propriety persecuted them, stripped reality of myth, attacked them, or better yet, ignored them.

Are they the hawk or the deer, these sad benighted souls in the 27 Club?

"The wounded deer leaps highest," the poem goes, Emily felt the connection, desperation, adrenalin—a paroxysm of purpose, lifeblood dedicated to a last-ditch effort to realize its *raison d'etre.* Every muscle, sinew, fiber in a deer's being that leaps, to preserve life, escape the shot—death never takes a vacation.

Or are they the hawk? There's often enough a vivid,

violent transgression, a new artist breaking ground, displacing the old, showing confidence, strength. There's a revolution in sensibility often enough, a bold strike by what will be on what is, that seems weak and old to the wild what will be. There's a new sensibility, new vision, new art, fresh from the House of Mystery. The House of Propriety seems run down, decrepit, in comparison. Or a shabby vestige, a shell, when new life breaks free. New eggs replace the fossils anyway. But the fossils have the police.

There's blood sport in new vision, replacing the old, there's the hawk at play. Or maybe it's the same old dance, on the killing floor, the singer must die, long live the singer. Orpheus, Eurydice.

XXXI

Up from the underground…The march of civilization with blood on our face, smoke in our nostrils. The fresh-faced college kids joking around, with snide remarks to acquaintances, not one of them, not in their group. Intent on growing careers, in the great American drama. Alienation and synthesis, repulsion and incorporation, til we're all mad, assailing opportunists in Brook Bros. suits, claiming and scrapping for our place in the sun. Trampling in the dust whatever is retrograde, lingering, not quick enough. Obliterate memory, history. It's progress, but it's going the wrong way.

Out on the streets in America. Few walk anymore, they race around in their suicide machines, their glory engines, intent on having a great summer. Do spring break debauches in St. Lauderdale, come back and press their nose to the grindstone, no one will ever know, outside of a small circle of friends. Maybe in a computer file on their iPad, a midlevel dark web, not for *Facebook*, so we integrate the devil and angel.

Everybody loves the sharks. Fans pouring into the building tonight, for the Stanley Cup playoffs. Vanity of vanity saith the preacher, all is vanity. If they win tonight they go to the championship, the first time in 25 years. Interviewing the captain, who says confidently, "we learn..."

The ¾ orange moon over the traffic and treetops magnetizes the moment, and captures my imagination.

Like a giant I went striding down the streets, on foot, through the parks, over the meadows and fields, my legs the size of buildings, my arms larger than tree trunks, for a moment, seeing the beautiful sadness of the dumb, blind, moaning, hot, wet, wild earth, and man's artifacts and constructions, creations, built to preserve and protect, to insulate and propagate, our self-preserving energies devoted to slaving our preservations, producing and consuming, on and on.

The women's softer faces in a lighted window, or beckoning down hallways, the nest-makers, the nest-preservers, God bless them, companions to our heart's sorrow and toils, aspirations and dreams, the right faces of the children on their way to school, climbing onto the bus, how much they know, trailing clouds of immortality behind, and how little, growing into their manacles, with stops and starts, in fits, inevitably, maturing to take their place among the consumer and producers.

For a moment it seemed I could touch the sky with my hand, and rip off the façade, these stars twinkling above the streets and buildings, imperial, forlorn majesty, or distinct, close, lights from a distant fire magnetizing our faces, renewed in our faces, in a transmitted form.

Who be the ringmaster, in the circus, who the barker, on the fairground, the captain on the ship? Surely a game, a gamut, a test, we each were taking, an inscrutable end, the wild, inchoate sadness of it all, a rollercoaster ride in rough seas, ears dumb to all but the screaming, feathery our nests.

I was about serious work. I was on a mission from God, was here to draw blood, and dip my pen in it, and carry on, in a sensual procreating impulse, aspirations to the divine, amid my sodden details, transgressions, violence in the world, violence in my mind, there I said it, and laughter all around me. An ongoing house of trials, with unbearable masked figures, on their way.

Postscript

25 years later. H. went back to school and became a lawyer, with a degree in environmental law. For awhile he worked for a solar power company, drawing up contracts. Currently, he works for the State of California, helping them enforce their clean air policies, the strictest in the nation.

Joseph went back to school and received a PhD in English Literature. After much soul searching, and leg work, he secured an assistant professorship at a well known Ivy League university. He married Anna, and they have two children together, Savannah and Mark.

3
The Bridge

All kinds of coincidences pop up in life, and it is difficult to tell if they mean anything or what. It is probably better not to know. I can sense sometimes the foot on the lip of something big, and I am actually glad to be in the dark about what it is, or just may be. Some things I do not even want to hear about.

I had been working for *Amtam* about two years when I met Mirra. I am a mechanical engineer. I have an M.A. in business Administration as well. I suppose I consider myself fairly well ensconced in my little niche at *Amtam*. I was pulling down a cool 90 Gs, which is not bad, and the work went from miserable to fair, but that was work, and there was nothing much that you could do about that. I met Bernard almost exactly the time I met Mirra. They had been wining and dining him, and cooing pretty nothings in his ear, and I had heard our new division chief was going to make Mallick look like an amateur, though I always kind of liked Mallick, even if he did always wear a rumpled sports jacket, and talked like he had marbles in his mouth. Holo Lukoloa loved himself. Holo Lukoloa thought he was hot, and the people under him had to be hot. The way he treated Bernard totally confirmed it in my mind, and it was this minor revelation *Amtam* sent me, through their treatment of Bernard, that propelled me into a mood so foul, and yet so helpless, a mood so toxic, and yet as I well realized, so futile, that Mirra just happened to spin into. And somewhere it is all connected, the way I took to her. And somehow it is all almost expected, predictable, in fact. But that's where I get onto the lip of something I'm not sure I want to know about, like I said and—forget it.

I was on the *Amtam* medical plan, and I was due for an appointment. The sleek, well-groomed asian man, Dr. Hoy, welcomed me in. I had been sitting in the potted plants, flipping *National Geographics* only ten minutes, a new record (but hey, no skin off my back, I was there on company time.)

I had seen her, she had flickered like a small, blond flame from the hidden chambers, and bringing files to the receptionist, whispered something making the receptionist guffaw (the receptionist was a large, roughhewn lesbian, so it seemed), and had floated on that boisterous guffaw back from the lioness to the hidden, the zones where patients stripped and waited and all veneers the tests firmly but beneficently peeled, and I thought nothing much. Dr. Hoy sent me to x-ray on feeling out my knee. Weekend softball, a fly ball to left field, I pursue it and wrench my knee in a molehill, or something, and each time I applied pressure since that day (three months at that point, at least), a needle stabbed me, from my knee up to my thigh. Not only did it not get better, it got distinctly worse. I walked down to x-ray, and Mirra greeted me briskly, and sat me down, and brought one of those lead pads, and put it on my lap, and smiled, this won't take a minute she said. She smiled again. I leaned back and looked around. It was just a small, square room with the big x-ray machine, and its crane, and pea-soup eye. And she looked like an ant with a crumb too big for her as she swung it into place over my knee. She scooted out of the room. I heard that electric hum. I knew all about x-ray machines. I had helped build one. She came out and asked me if everything was okay just as I was summoning up the blueprints. Sure, I nodded. She came over and adjusted the protective lead.

Maybe it was the little fractional instant of extra time she took, adjusting the armor on my laps, maybe it was her perfume, which was delicate, but definite, maybe it was the hint of a smile barely suppressed, or the hint of a lack of a smile, under an apparent smile, I do not know, but for the first time I saw her. She looked good. She was small, delicate, lissome. She could not have weighed more than 110 pounds. She had a long neck. Her curly, almost whitish blond hair hung with girlish curls down around her shoulders and when she turned her hair swung with her, so her turn was something larger than herself, an event. I forgot about the blueprints. How are you today?, she asked me. Fine, I replied. I do not engage in stupid conversation unless business requires. She came over and adjusted the padding again, and this time wiggled a little as she left to take the second shot. That'll do it, Mr. Barry, she informed me, after the second round. I left, and returned to work, and the day Bernard was fired I called Dr. Hoy's office and asked to talk to her. I identified myself, and she recalled me, and seemed friendly enough. I remember I was munching a chicken leg I had a habit of filching from the cafeteria at the time. She agreed to go with me Saturday night, to have dinner at the *Jefferson Bar and Grill*. I kissed the receiver and it smelled like chicken.

The dinner went well enough. We made it at her

apartment afterwards. We smoked cigarettes after sex. I have a cat. I said I had to get back to feed my cat. It started off freely and easily enough. I would not have believed if someone told me six months later because of her I would have committed an assault and battery, succumbed to witchcraft, committed arson, and for a few terrible, terrific seconds, (and this is what is most shameful), attempted to strangle my sister.

We began seeing each other two to three times a week. We didn't talk that much. I talk with plenty of people at work. I didn't care to talk to her. I suppose I was trying to keep something I had hidden intact and make sure myself I did not forget where I had hid it. She seemed to like the sex. I seemed to like the sex. Period.

Something was bothering me, I was losing something, and I was like a swimmer with something which all of a sudden grabbed onto his leg, leeched onto his leg, and was pulling him down. I did not know what it was. The way they treated Bernard pissed me off. Then that skywalk which collapsed (not that I had anything to do with it collapsing, but I did work on that project.)

The fact it was a construction rather than a design defect relieved Holo and us all, but it still bugged me. I don't know why it bugged me but it did. It was something having to do with this. They wined and dined Bernard, a sweet guy, a gem, they made him an offer and he quit a fine, nice, secure job with *Larens*, to come work for *Amtam*. Holo Lukoloa (his father was Hawaiian) was preening himself on his catch. He apparently had taken a real hankering to Bernard's wife, she was a knockout, though it sounds like she would have none of Holo. Bernard was fired two weeks after he came to work for *Amtam*. Two frigging weeks. Why you can't figure out if a fellow can use a pocket calculator in two weeks. Bernard was bounced, and he lost everything. From Florida to California he had come, on promises from Holo. Pulled his two kids out of school. Moved his grandmother from a Florida nursing home to a California one. Kissed his old good salary, kissed his old good workplace, kissed his old good way of life goodbye. And for what? Holo Lukaloa, and his promises. Holo Lukaloa, and sweet nothings. Maybe just Holo Lukaloa and Holo's hopes to make it with Bernard's filly. I saw Bernard the day he left. Why had they fired him?, I asked. They didn't tell me, he said. They don't have to. Of course it is true, we are working without contracts, and our employer has the right to terminate "at will." Bernard smoked cigarettes and looked out my 23rd story window like he wanted to jump. Will you stay in California? Who knows?, he replied. I haven't had a lot of luck here so far. We said goodbye, and he vanished out of my life, like an unpleasant dream. I asked Holo about it later. He was slow on the paper work, Holo said. Slow on the paperwork, he was here two weeks Holo, Jesus Christ. Holo smoked cigars and he had this disgusting habit I despised, dropping his ash without caring. He was surveying his imagined kingdom from my window, the very window Bernard had looked like he wanted nothing more than to jump out of two weeks earlier, and he flicked some ashes on the begonias. I could hear them hit the soil as they hissed. This is not a charity kid, it's a business, he snarled and walked out. I was left saying "you prick" to a picture of the Golden Gate Bridge. Bernard's wife had told Holo where to get off. Holo's little bid, I could see. Now if you are nice to me, he would say to her, well I'll be nice to Bernard. It's as simple as that. I just wish she would have kicked him in the balls, but people like Holo Lukoloa always live to fight another day. Then that day or the next, the headlines screamed the falling catwalk, and the hundreds that had died. It was a bad week. And more than that was bad. Something in me was bothered, really bothered. You know, the workplace is external, you sever it from your personal life, it is the only sensible thing to do, but it was getting harder and harder to sever. What I did and how I spend my hours, and the way I spend my hours, in the light of the firing of Bernard, and the falling catwalk, began to take its toll. I clung to Mirra I suppose negotiating these once innocent waters, now revealing unknown and dangerous reefs hiding just beneath the calm, metronomic surfaces.

I started waking up screaming in the middle of the night, and be out the door, without even remembering putting my clothes on. A nameless terror had seized me. Something without even form, had taken possession of my imagination, and turned everything. I saw things in a precise, ghastly light I had never seen them before. A disgusting grand Bach organ of horror dominated my sleepless hours. The nine to five I had honed still functioned, though it functioned on the edge of this isle of unspeakableness, and I strove to sever whatever it was that came to roost, from the business of day to day and picking up the checks.

My sister Latta had followed me, when I had moved out to the west coast, by two years. She lived an hour south, and I used to drive to see her once monthly at most, or she would drive to see me. I began driving every week to see her now. She was getting over a disastrous affair, a serious relationship. She was only 23. She described the guy and told me about the guy. She needed badly to talk about it. I told her nothing of myself, but gladly listened to her.

The guy's name was Robert. He worked for Hughes Aircraft. He was a doll. Tall, blond, good-looking. Good-looking like me, I wanted to know, my curiosity piqued. At least she replied, if not better.

So why do you like him? I wanted to know. I had been married. It had lasted two years. But I did not think I had ever been in love. I had a hot time with the women before I was married. To be married was a drag. That same gluppy kitchen table, that same boring conversation, which Jojo, my wife, seemed particularly to love, to depend on. It left me bored stiff. I hate predictability. I had enough predictability at my job. Doing the laundry together Sunday morning, and drinking the beer and watching the game, what a bore, Sunday afternoon. Bowling with John and Sue. Visits to the in-laws. Talk about kids when the same conversations, and same predictable Jojo bored me stiff. She was marvelous, a great person, no question about it. A great person.

Anyway, she said she loved him. Why?, I wanted to know. Passion was a mystery, like a lagoon I saw through a telescope, but had never explored.

My sister kept me up nights telling me why. She had been an old maid, and with Robert she was a woman. Robert went wind-surfing and was exciting. Robert tinkered with her car, and taught her stuff. Robert made her laugh. Robert was hot in bed. Robert made her feel like a woman. It went on and on. She really loved him. I was impressed. She wanted to know about Mirra. No big deal, I put her off. How's work? Eh, I replied. You seem bothered, Latta would say. She tried to pry my secrets out of me. I was not going for it. Not yet.

I fell out of touch with Mirra and had an affair with a woman I met at a bar. I told her I was a mechanical engineer. I'd like to see your diagrams, she cooed. We went to her place, and I left before dawn. I saw her once or twice, no big deal. I met Linda at work. She was a mechanical engineer called in to consult on a big project I was involved with. She wore a skirt, and kept showing me her thigh, as the talk went around the room. There were (myself excluded), six of us. Stevens, Bartholomew, Landau, from *Amtam*, and Christopher, Salem, and her. We laid the prints out on a table. She began kicking my shin under the table with her high heel and we made a date. I met her at the restaurant (in a disgusting pattern, too many times to count, I utilized the facilities of the *Jefferson* precisely for such purposes), and we made it at her apartment. I told her I had to leave to feed my cat. No big deal. I started thinking of Mirra, when the bad dreams started. At least, that is how I see it now. She was very understated, underspoken. Something was there I could not put my finger on. My life was getting away from me, and my dreams were a sign of that, and I could not put my finger on that either. Maybe Mirra could. A mystery had intervened, had separated me from both these things. I called her apartment for days. No answer. I called Dr. Hoy's office. The receptionist refused to reveal Mirra's new work number. Brick wall! And I thought women were giving! Finally, I squeezed out where she worked.

I called Mirra, and she acted like I was a stranger, which is basically what I was. I had not stayed at Mirra's once. I've switched jobs, she told me. She worked now as a respiratory therapist, at St. Bonaventure Hospital, a very large private hospital. She had been going to school for four years part time, I had not even known. I knew little about her, I realized. One night we were eating dinner, by candlelight, and she had said, you must have a lot of women chasing your heels. Why?, I wanted to know. You know, she had retorted. No I don't, I said. Tell me. Well, you're good looking, you're a hunk, basically. Am I?, I had said amused, hiding a vanity which was sizable, in spite of myself. Oh come on, she had said, a bit disgusted with me. I liked that tinge of disgust with which she had dismissed me, she was honest, she was perceptive, she wanted something from me, and maybe now I wanted something back. I want to see you, I got to see you, today, I had insisted. Where are you? Why aren't you ever home? Then she said words that hit my heart. I'm seeing someone, that's why. I stay at his house. I'm coming over I said, and hung up.

We made love in the janitor's closet, standing up.

(Smell of pine-sol and ammonia not recommended.) Did the Virgin Mary come off like a nurse?

I wanted to see her badly. I told her that over the phone, and in person. She was seeing some jerk. What was his name? Robert. What did he do? He worked for *Hughes*. Where did he live? Santa Rosa. What? Could it be, I wondered flabbergasted, the guy that had dumped, and who my sister had dumped. Impossible!

The Robert you knew, why did you split with him, I called and drilled my sister. I thought you loved him. Well, I do, sort of, she confessed. Then why split?, I demanded. Well, we had differences. What differences? He wasn't ready for marriage, I was. He was too macho, too. And basically, he wanted to play the field. His father was a drunk, to boot. He wanted his father to move in with us, if we lived together. No way. So you dumped him? Sort of. Does he still love you? Maybe, probably. It doesn't matter. We have mutual friends. He is seeing someone named Mirra. Listen Tina, I'm going to tell you an incredible story now. (My childhood nickname for Latta was Tina).

I went out for a walk, screaming at the moon. I needed Mirra badly. My dreams were getting more and more drastic. I had never paid much attention to my dreams, but I could not get through the day without a sort of flashing image of these things which before had always seemed to keep in place. My sister was incredulous. I told her my plan. At first she refused but I begged her, I made a total fool of myself, and she must have been ashamed, because she finally consented.

I walked in a whirl past the buildings in the night. A three-quarter moon peered over the rooves sheepishly, as if having no business among the edifices. I saw the lights burning, and heard the cars roaring. I had always taken it for granted. Now I wondered where it was going, what it was doing, what it was for. I had the idea someone was looking for me. Around EACH CORNER I turned, I expected someone, a woman to call my name, but of course none was. Everything seemed mysterious, insoluble, enigmatic, slightly disquieting, whereas everything had made sense or seemed to, up to that point. The point was I had never wanted anything before, and now I wanted Mirra. Another half of the puzzle I was a part of was beyond my grasp though perhaps not indefinitely, and I was straining and striving to attain something, I know not for what reason. A gift was waiting. At each corner I rounded I hoped, no, I EXPECTED someone, perhaps Mirra to be there. It was a cool night, I walked without a jacket. I turned and saw a woman in a scarf of slender frame, and my heart leaped in my throat. Some guy came out and joined her, and looked me over as I walked past. Who were these people, I wondered, as I strode by in a whirl? Can it be there are so many of you, flitted through my brain. I had the sensation we were in a tunnel moving towards a light, which kept receding. Somehow I had made my way down to where I worked. The wharfs were nearby. The bridge gleamed almost supernaturally in the distance. I recalled as a child my fascination for bridges. I used to beg my father to buy puzzle books, connect-the-dots, with bridges. You'll be an architect someday, he would tell me, and so I was, or nearly. But now it was I who was the bridge. I was carrying something but I did not know what, I did not know why, and I did not know where. I was a transmitter, I was a ship. But what was my cargo? All I knew was I needed Mirra, because something had happened I had to share with her. And what had happened? Bernard? The collapsing skywalk? It had catalyzed some ticking time bomb, and I walked half-expecting to find her form sheer desire.

A strange period began, I cannot tell. Only lately is the dank almost narcotic effluvium of this period wearing off; yes, I think it is finally wearing off. My sister wrote to Robert begging him to return. The thrust of her letter was she loved him, whether his father was a wino or not, whether he was macho or not, whether he wanted to play the field or not, and that was the Lord's truth. She wrote this letter for me, she later confessed, as she began it, but she concluded it in her own name, and meant every word of it. I met Robert when I visited Mirra at work. He was a tall, blond athletic sort, not unlike myself. I hated him immediately. He knew about me too apparently. Mirra was the embarrassed host. We stood talking about the weather, the news, the stock market, the hospital business, as each of us eyed Mirra's voluptuous, winsome lithesomeness beneath her white, before she fled on emergency, and we were left with just the naked truth.

As I saw my reflection, so it seemed, standing opposite me, and we talked about the latest sex scandal and the public life of a politician, as we discoursed on anonymity for an ax murderer, shielded by a state law in a public hospital, guaranteeing the privacy of mental health records; and the stress of jet-lag which hit air travelers, and was apparently now a documented scientific fact; I wondered what I had been doing with my life. This man opposite me could have been my double. He resembled me like a brother. He seemed pathetic. I, not he, would have the rights to Mirra's body. I, not he, would win Mirra and share Mirra's dream, and partake in Mirra's world. I, not he, would share with Mirra the resources of the heart, and feed her, and take care of her when times got rough.

All my life I had been rational, calculating, practical. I had been reared to be prepared, logical, pragmatic. I cannot tell you of the power of these dreams. It was as if I had designed the catwalk that had fallen.

A tremendous guilt crowded the edges of this dream. Faceless figures walked up to me and pointed their fingers at me from the safety of hoods. My parents are Mormons, and I, as my sister, was raised a Mormon. Money is an honorable thing. There is no shame in making money. Money is Mommy. It is a virtue in our creed. I saw my parents at a grand fete, at a great, a renowned hotel. Everyone was there. The chief of police. The fire commissioner. The mayor himself. And I was guest of honor. For it was I who built the magnificent hotel, I who planned the psalm to money, to corporate muscle, to progressive architectural soundness, and it was I who appeared as guest of honor.

The band struck up a waltz. The mayor, the police chief, the fire commissioner took the floor. My parents cajoled me, but I refused, preferring the sidelines, a pretty girl waited for me to ask her to dance but I declined, preferring to revel in the fun the others had, and basking in the honor they bestowed. After all, it was my company's money. And it was my company's position and wherewithal which had landed the bid. But it was my labor. My work, my design. I was the author of the creation so grand. The collapsing skywalk seemed to collapse underwater. Most I recall the look of utter surprise, not even fear, on the guests dancing within the arches.

'London Bridge is falling down
falling down, falling down
London Bridge is falling down
my fair lady.'

I called my parents constantly in the next few weeks, and they assured me of their health. I had to see Mirra since I felt I was going mad. I had to get rid of that idiot Robert, and I logical, pragmatic, practical, called on an unusual man, a sculptor of my acquaintance from the West Indies, and bought clay, of substantial quality, pins, and a live chicken.

I would do voodoo. That is how I would get rid of him.

I had always been good with my hands. I had always loved, since a little child, fashioning, shaping things. Little did I think I would ever turn my talents in the direction the nightlife witnessed me turning them almost aglee, and with mad enthusiasm now.

There I was, bent over in the witching hour, the hours

saved for dream, except I was scared to sleep because the dreams that came terrified me so, especially the look of amazement in my mother's eyes that went beyond even reproach, so I did not sleep, my dream was life, since life became a dream, and I worked on fashioning a replica of Richard, my very double. (Richard, Robert, whoever.) Now in retrospect, I see I was mad. Our criminal justice system does not account voodoo a crime. Apparently a *mens rea* (mental intent), is needed, and not only, but an *actus reus* (act of crime) is needed, and sticking pins in an effigy or likeness of a competitor is according to American jurisprudence not sufficient *actus reus* to be bound. I could stick all the pins in Richard's model as I wanted, and wished, until my heart's content. And so I did. 3 a.m., 4 a.m... The city is sleeping. Silence is all around. At most, an alley cat scurries across a rooftop, mating on a dare. The biggest decision in my life those days was where to stick Richard, where would do him quickest in. I did not mind killing him, but I wondered if that would be quickest. My main priority was to eliminate him from the scene, so Mirra would be mine. I knew nothing of Mirra, I realized. Had she been married? Where was she from? Did she have children?

She had a worldly, hard-won maturity, despite her youthfulness, which was what MAY HAVE well drawn me, as a superior metal, an inferior metal to its side. Maybe she was a mother. I had no idea, was past caring. All I knew was that she was the key to the door, the map to the trove, the resolution of the question mark my work, my very life, had added up to lay. I needed to sleep next to someone who would listen to my heart, and make it calm, and make it sing.

I worked on the doll steadily. I decided to stick the groin area. I reasoned problems there would more quickly end the serenade they had. Meanwhile, depending on a double whammy, I nightly called my sister. She and Richard were passing through their own night of fire, apparently. They were in the midst of a blazing affair. Richard loved her. And yet, according to my sister, did not trust her yet, and so clung to Mirra as armory against a woman who had ditched him when he loved. And so it was a stalemate.

The night seemed to expand, and a circle widened. The world became newer, and wilder than it was. I bought live chickens, from a farm outside the city, one by one. I slaughtered it, and let the blood run according to the custom. Once I caught a glimpse of a shadow, and it was pouring blood into a cup, and making signs, and sticking pins into a doll. I laughed like a maniac and continued my awful work. My sister informed me Richard couldn't get it up with her, and could not stand to see her anymore, because she had broken his heart. My dreadful work had backfired, apparently. Mirra was never at home the nights I called.

I was closed out of Mirra's life, and my obsession was a puzzle to her, though I confessed I loved her on the phone. I went looking for her at the hospital and found her with Richard. Something snapped. I jumped on my double, so suave, so self-assured. I wanted to murder that very suavity, that very self-assurance.

Mirra really swatted me with a frying pan. The arresting officer was an attractive female (gay, it seemed to me) named Maureen. I was booked for assault and battery. (Richard it turned out refused to press charges so I walked.) What humiliation! What degradation! Lee Michaels, my immediate superior from *Amtam* came down, and brought a lawyer. Lee never breathed a word to Holo for which I am sincerely grateful. They slapped a temporary restraining order on me, and I was barred from visiting Mirra at her home, or at the hospital. I spent only one night in jail, but in one night a person can do a lot of thinking. It has taken months to put it together, and I am putting it together still.

I did voodoo on my double: I wanted to incapacitate my double!

2

All I wanted to do was to talk with Mirra. But she refused to talk to me. I had a week vacation coming up at *Amtam*, and it could not have come at a better time. Tina implored me over and over again to go away, visit someone, a friend, our parents, just get away. She was right, I really did need to get away, and I decided to seek my parents, and forget about everything for awhile.

My mom and dad live in a suburb called Clearview, a few miles outside of Salt Lake City. My dad is a big insurance executive, and my mom is a computer programmer. I was pleasantly smashed when I got off the plane, because the stewardess (a red-head with red fingernails, sultry lips, and green eye makeup) kept coming by offering drinks, and I kept accepting, and she kept coming by, and I kept accepting.

And then I was home, home in the very house I had grown up in, home where I brought my first date, after the movie, home where I smashed the car, and my allowance was suspended for a year, home of first feats, and home of baby talk, and much more, it was good to be home.

I was almost treated like a wounded person. Tina must have let them in on something, I did not. My dad arranged our outings practically hour by hour, day by day. My mom would bake me, besides all the great meals, breads, and cakes, and she would come talk to me, and practically tuck me in at night. I heard all these tales from my childhood, adolescence, fondly recalled, fondly remembered. It gave me a sense of place in the universe, like I had a home somewhere.

My dad and I went sailing on his schooner, we went clear water fishing, we played golf. Sammy, a 40 year old black man was our caddy at the course, and he would say stuff like, "looks like a 4 iron Mr. Barry, hmm?" The golf course was beautiful, we played bathed in a wondrous sunset, a magic gold light, and in the end it seemed almost unbearably sad, we had to leave, like saying goodbye to an enchanted isle, we could not be certain would remain.

Meanwhile, I was having fervent, mad conversations with Mirra, who apparently cared for me a great deal, but was frightened of me simultaneously, and because of this, repulsed by me. I saw the pony she was 1,000 miles from me, and wanted to kiss her so bad, she was the lifeline, I

99

had never felt like this before. I had a dream about her, and I told her. I was in some sort of institutional building, either a barracks or a hospital, maybe both, and there was a bright light, and all of a sudden I was on a subway platform, running for a train, and I saw her in front of me, running too. Did we make the train?, she asked. I do not know, I cannot remember, I said. I found out about her. Mirra grew up in the east end of St. Louis, with four brothers and sisters. The wolf was always at the door. Her father worked in a factory, and when he came home he tended to get drunk. She went to a community college, put her shoulder to the wheel, and after transferring earned her degree in biology. Her mother died of cancer when Mirra was in college, another wolf at the door.

She had taken communion, and lapsed Catholic or not, would often go to church in times of trouble. She felt uplifted there enough, and would ask the heavens to hear her in prayer. I talked to her, and she talked to me, for the first time. We talked not only of acts, but dreams, not only of histories, but of desires. I woke up one morning, thrilled I had no more dreams of skywalks, and had not once thought of Bernard, and saw blood dripping from the walls, I told her, but it was not a scary blood, it was a good blood, maybe blood that has to flow when life itself does change. We rang off by sending hot kisses through the wire.

I was sure I was recovering. That madness on the coast was just an aberration. And just to be sure, and keep it together, I would, as Mirra had repeatedly suggested, see a shrink.

I left two days later. Two incidents stand out in my mind. First, my dad has a smoker and when that meat cooked it came out so tender, it had a wild taste, moist, and with a subtle flavoring of smoke. One day when my parents were out I put out a pork roast, thawed it, and built a large fire in the charcoal tray. In my absentmindedness, I put the water tray on before the fire had settled, put the pork on the rack, covered it with a hood, and then went shopping for champagne. It was my last day, I wanted to cook them a nice meal. Water-smoking was a snap, so I thought. I got back an hour later, and managed to put out a fire. Flames were leaping three or four feet out of the hood. That was number one.

My mom came home. My dad came home. I carved off the char, and what lay beneath was delicious. We had a great meal. This is number two. We ate staring out at the singed hood, and puddles on the patio where I had doused the fire. Neither of them said a word about it. (But that is the way my family is, unless something is good, they do not even want to know.)

"Go to church," my mother advised, "it'll uplift you" she said, hugging me farewell.

My dad drove me to the airport. While he loved me, I sensed he would be relieved when I had left. Well, so would I. Get me home to Mirra, I commanded, as I boarded the plane. All I wanted to do was love her up good.

I was pleasantly smashed when I landed. I had been gone only one week. And yet in that one week much had happened. Tina and Mirra told me of it, at the airport. We were one big happy family. It was all settled. Robert was with Tina. Mirra was with me. Robert liked me. Tina liked Mirra. Tina loved me. Two months have passed since that buccolic greeting.

At *Amtam*, work proceeds apace. Holo is still the idiot, a sort of perfect symmetrical idiot. Lee and I joke about him, in our spare time. That is good. And sometimes at *Amtam* I sit and worry Mirra will get hit by a car. Or I worry some guy will walk up to her and shoot her. At this point I do not know what I would do without her.

Something remains, and I want very badly to tell it. And it has to do with a day I waited in an old green car with my dad, at the railroad track, and a freight train was rolling down the track, and a man on a horse, in one of those English style get-ups, came clopping to a halt beside us. I could not have been more than six. The horse was a dazzling, majestic animal, it danced and pranced, and then it heard this train. The train chugged on the other side of the bend, so one could hear a noise like thunder and see nothing. Fear splashed the horse's spirit. It bucked, reared, it foamed at the mouth. No emotion I was cognizant of as a child crossed the rider's face. The rider reined, aloof, cheerful, and he brought the horse back down each time it reared, and he sunk his will into it, and forced the horse to stand its ground. The train put on the brakes, and the cars rebounded with a heavy metal clash, like the knocking of fearful, unappeasable gods, and the horse splayed its hooves and shot like an arrow in the air. The man held on, blood poured from the horse's side. Again and again, the rider in that same spot dug his spurs into the horse's flank. Finally the train passed by, and the indomitable rider, and the bleeding horse galloped off.

I have been pragmatic, logical. I have lived my life in a line straight as any I draft for our company's clients. The nights I went crazy, the night, or something, opened up. There is more than one kingdom. Someone has been doing voodoo on me.

I look back aghast at the events of that shocking week. Could I have been mad? I must have been mad! What other explanation for when I climbed up the fire-escape and into Mirra's apartment while she laughed in the bedroom with Richard, humming "Scheherazade," and I commenced quietly gathering newspapers. I struck a match and tried to burn the place down. And what can I be but flabbergasted too, and ashamed, how ashamed, when, convinced my sister was not trying ferociously enough to win her ex back, I leaped at her throat, foaming at the mouth, as she later described it, and threw her to the ground in a frenzy. I was somewhere else. Blame it on the moon. Blame it on Holo Lukoloa. Blame it on the divided kingdom. And still, to this day, I see Holo Lukoloa emerge, like Bogart from a mist, and say "kid, I've been hearing rumors...nasty rumors...If you were to lose the Borensen account kid...well, that would be it, you know..."

Will I go mad? I will not go mad. I will go to work, that's the only place I will go. Mirra takes my face in her hands, and wipes the sweat from my brow. Between me and Lukoloa and the collapsing catwalk, and God knows what other madness, stands Mirra. I know it. She knows it. And I swear someday I will do the same for her. I cannot wait for that day to come to show her how much I love her, because we have created a contract, a living bond, and I'll be blasted if I do not get to repay her, because she is an angel.

Needles were jabbed into my eyes. Needles were jabbed into my ears.

I am that horse, and it never fought its way out of the hatching, out of the egg. I am the rider, and always, as if born with that very spur on my foot, that very bridle, very rein, I have wielded a calm, authoritative control with savage precision, a relentless, mechanical control. And I am diminished from it. And I am the less for it. And alas, even Mirra, bright face, precious, unthinkable Mirra, is but a palliative. And tomorrow I go to work. And on that train which rolls in my dreams, which daylight says put from my mind, I can hear the clanking, abraiding cars, I can hear the unrelaxed, mechanical, repulsive, relentless cars, as I apply the spurs, a phallus, rending the horse's flank, over and over, and I wake up screaming. What would I do without Mirra? Where would I be without Mirra? And I will tell you what those metal cars ceaselessly rolling past like a nauseating, unending dream are carrying, horse meat. And soon I will kiss Mirra goodbye, and soon I will check in, and that's alright. Just no more faces of Bernard.

Just no more collapsing skywalks. Lighten up, that is the secret. I have to lighten up. Picture Mirra, Mirra is the shining light. A work place could never be other than a work place. And while the glass is half-empty, it is also half-full.

I wanted to build a rainbow bridge. I wanted to be something more than a hand hired to build defective skywalks.

One day Mirra took me to the library. I remembered engineering school days, studying for finals. Libraries are a drag.

Mirra took my hand and read me a poem written on the library wall.

> *Books*
> *delight-us*
> *speak-to-us*
> *counsel-us*
> *and-are*
> *joined-to-us*
> *as-it-were*
> *by-a-loving*
> *and-active*
> *relationship.*

"Look, there's a mother teaching her child to read. Let's start a family. Wouldn't it be wonderful?" My heart melted.

Weeks are passing. Life is calming down. Mirra is calming down. I am calming down. An unexpected richness enters in. It really does appear like we have the volts, the care, and the desire to make it. Mirra and I go for long walks together. I tend to lead us to the water, somehow we end up always near the water. I have begun to feel what it means to be alive. She is an arrow, beyond herself for me, and I for her. We stand in the starlight, and we are starlight, we are composed of star desires, star dreams, tender star glimmerings, we are a circulation of sunlight and starlight paddling past our own expectations and imaginings. We roar with the tigers, yelp with the fireflies. Her tender, precious face in a star mirror comes streaming through. With her I am bound on a living wheel, touched by a living flame. People look at us strangely as we pass, so in love. I for her, she for me, and each beyond ourselves in part of a living mystery partaking, and giving, so we pass. I feel good things are coming our way. (Where had I been all this time? I did not remember to remember). And I feel under that starlight, near the water, we may be a crossing over. Yet who knows, six months from now, this entire scene could well be rearranged. One of the hardest things seems to be to change. Yet for now, the great, laughing starlight doors of her face are open, and I step through. The mermaid that she is waits on the other side, like a future. I was not born to be Lot's wife. Once Lady Luck gives one the go, there will be no looking back. Hard work gets one to the door. Grace provides the key. Lady Luck lends us some horses, and we are off.

Six months have passed since last I picked up these pages. I am still with Mirra. Unbelievable! And yet it is also hard to imagine one time I was not with Mirra! And remember that receptionist? I bought her roses!

4
Those Who Wait

1

This is how it begins. Vast stretches, deserts crossed by black winds nursing plagues, luminous highways under brittle stars, articulate mounts. Fires spot dark hills under a broken moon. Wolves crouch in blue undergrowth where delicate fawns eat flowers, skitter playfully down paths. Communities of snails, crickets in hidden places, move like patterns over a green floor, fatal as the tide...

He sees women lean from balconies, gaze into distances, lucid and tranquil. Children throw stones along the river, laugh in the sun. A pale girl waves to distant boats.

Then footsteps in forests, resonant echoes in the warm spring air. At dawn he holds a leaf between his fingers, scents hanging like premonitions behind trees. As he progresses smells form like clouds in his mind, diffuse; certain events in future like charges about which these histories to later accumulate, consolidate anew. No storm is too large for his mouth. Forests increase his appetite. Blushing, he dons the blue clothe of the sky like a woman dons a gown. Drunk, he sleeps.

2

White crystalline skies, like the image on a roll of negatives. Endlessness of gray fields under a setting sun. Faint breezes, dry as dust, make slow circles around the youth's body, drop exhausted to his feet. Gray horizons expel shadows of bird's wings husking through dusk solidities, plummeting.

Out of a corner of the scene emerges a second figure who glides across large distances with incredible facility. He passes within perhaps 20 yards of the youth, continuing in a straight line, like a magnetized toy in a slot. His arms hang at his side motionless, and seem in no way connected to or dependent on his body. He vanishes quickly into the opposite horizon but leaves behind a trail of silver crystals suspended in the wake of his body, tracers on a photoelectric plate. The sun droops at the bottom of the sky, a red flower encased in front, finally disappears. A dark, splintered blueness seeps into spaces but the trail remains unaffected, shooting out like a silver arrow into the night...

Days without impact, nights without dreams. Crippled winds with broken backs collapse around the youth as he walks. He kicks at them tentatively with the toe of his boot, causing them to tinkle mildly like bags full of shattered glass. Far off, birds to frozen skies are nailed.

In the nighttime wan stars twinkle through the hollow of a blue, silent horn. Out of absence of event, and absence of most fundamental basic gestures creeps organic torpor, subtle lassitudes. Then a period follows where dreams, desires, memories are deposited like eggs to hatch in gray atmospheres, after which to be consumed by gaunt insides. Conic illuminations, mind matter particulars, singing blood, hospital flesh, cavort in open fields, resurrected from dusty tombs of sequence, order, proportion. Traumas spin like dervishes through meadows, whipping up shadows of winds, that jump with spectral precision on open nerves, then terminate themselves with inklings and contemplation upon reaching gale force.

Scenes charged with tremendous significance unroll like old movies across the sky. Gaseous eggs burst with loud hissing noises as the youth sucks at the contents through slender straws. (Multicolored shells remain which fade into morning.) For a period of time he walks enclosed, lost in an effluvium of pink thoughts and green weather, a larval entity, experiencing movements like flowers, mystical glimmerings of almost hypodermic intensity.

Later, the eggs and the incubus vanish inside him, like smoke down chimneys. The sky remains, crystalline, indifferent. Uneatable grains sway like aged dancers to faint, lost melodies whispering across plains. The silver arrow too remains, cryptic cipher.

3

Vast bleak bog whose borders fade into distance under crystal skies. Haze hangs low in branches, heavier than wind. Drab ravens cruise in and out of clouds, spectral, inevitable. To the ear, hum of marsh machinery, dull rumbles of power.

Great silver planes flying perpetually from fueling stop to fueling stop alight, like prehistoric birds on runways, take off again without destinations. Foul odors of tanks, intestinal tracts, float up enveloping everything in sick mists, non-specific fears. Hysteria of frightening resources in closed space is submerged in pathic calm.

Around capes, across bridges, over hills in midnights the youth comes. The arrow shoots through fog, all manners of obscurity, weirdly phosphorescent. The youth passes bizarre configurations in meadows, houses like engines, lawns like spikes, flowers with petal systems delicate as machinery, more secret than locks.

He spies ladders in the sun, and stars strewn across the sky, waiting to be gathered. Forests sway, a symphony of sadness. People pass. Musical notes drop from their mouths, settle softly onto floors.

Across rippling, unseeded expanse he goes, over territories dozing down corridors of minds. He sleeps in a vulture's shadow, near a gnarled trunk. He blinks awake in a low cloud, wanders off after the arrow...

4

Buildings down nighttimes which clutter and climb over each other like tin cans on a shelf. Somewhere, a gun goes off. He moves on, penetrates further. In the distance twang of faint guitars, lullabies drifting from windows.

In this section of the city, in some back room, under slowly turning fans, sit twelve persons. Some are old, some are young, women there as well as men, and they are all waiting.

They have been there ten minutes or for centuries, doing what they have been doing briefly, or even from before they were born. Red bugs cluster in corners, advance in tight formations across empty sections of

113

floor, regroup on other side, continue indefinitely.

There is one large rectangular table in the corner of the room, heaped with ashes, around which are situated the waiting twelve, in various attitudes suggesting hope, prayer, resignation. The youth enters. He is greeted by the man whose body has been the instrument of his arrival, and by the others as well. Thereafter, the stories begin. A clock rings from a tower but no one listens. It strikes twelve.

There are stories of all sorts.

1

The Boxer

"I gave it my best shot, for their applause and betting, the crowd was really hot, they were roarin' and sweating. My manager told me 10th round he had it in the bag unless I got lucky and he really got tagged. Mr. Manager Mr. Agent please don't take my bread, that's for me and my baby, we're gonna be wed. I'm the king of Vegas, I got ring rust on my knees, carry my pallet to the station, put me on that railroad heading east. I hit him with my right, I hit him with my left, I hit him with my head, 'cause there was nothing left. I'm the king of Vegas, I got ring rust on my knees, head full of rolling thunder, hey hey won't you dial my baby's number.

You want to fight, you want to fight? You want to brawl with me baby tonight? I'm the boxer. I come with my crown. You want to take it away from me, I'll make

114

you leave this town. I like your shorts. They're real cute. I'm a boxer baby. I'm gonna let you have my right and then my left.

They said I was out of my league right from the start, I showed them that a country boy has heart. I'm the king of Vegas, I got sawdust on my knees, carry my pallet to the station, put me on that railroad heading east.

I'm not sure where I am, I don't know my own mind, I'm lost in Vegas, at the corner of Knockout and Vine, a couple of years behind."

2

An Old One Speaks Up For A change

"I, who have swept across the floor of being, black-shoed, immaculate, a charade of broken gesture, sealed motions.

I, who discovered the shades inside the walls and shook them out, but now am lonely.

I, who am the shadow of my life, hand through a leaf, caught in machinery kitchen, disappearing rooms.

I, and the crisis nailed between forks, memories vanishing in brainpan.

I, and the yearning under the salad. And my eyes which have spilled out like water down my drain...

In the evening to stand out on porches, fire escapes, where insects hum towards light bulbs, fatally fascinated. To look angelic over grim, terrific buildings in the midnight, faces infused with memory glow. To sit doomed, passionless, wasted on stoops, dusty decades toppling in dreams.

Old lost men on benches, no hats, in conclusive downtown night. Loneliness telephones jangling in hallways. Shadows on our eyes. The moon rayed down through hardship bricks, windows, chalky and abstract."

She sits down, and another stands.

3

Roof Goer

I clamor up the iron nights, onto the rooftops, where the stars still exist. I receive messages from ancient history, and transmit them. And though it is done, and I am done, it nevertheless makes me feel like a creature who has just cause for his fleeting improvisations, his notable and energetic confusion.

Turning my eyes below, I bend my ear. From the radio tower of my dreams, desires, as heard from a distance, like the sea through a shell, I hear death. That which is around me is that which is in me, and that which I feel now will be felt entirely in the future, as long as there is commerce between our hearts and minds.

Though I am almost alone here, in my radio tower, I believe. I know that the snow could not fall so heavily if it doubted.

Those who stand on the rooftops across the buildings of the cities of the world, respect the stars. Respect the breeze, respect the vision. Look to whisper inarticulately but purely, if only at rare moments, look to appreciate the air. Lend credence to heartfelt utterances, soulful propaganda, obsolete mythologies strewn across the mind like constellations across the sky. Where closets close be inside them, and when they open publicize their secrets, so men might know them thoroughly and so see through them. At the center, where lovely songs go after entering the ear, go there too, the stars and fables meet. All hours, lovers meet.

Your hands attempt to silence your throat which, singing attempts to entrance your hands which are blind workers without a vision. Make peace between them, that is something difficult to do. I know what tunnels you go through, but say to you, 'do it.' In my mind, in my mind, I see you there, against the midnight, moving your hands to an invisible melody…"

His hands, which had been climbing through air, fall back to his side. He sits down.

4

A Woman Whose Cat Made A Break

"When I was younger, to look out over the hills and go mad in my mind. He stood beside me, he too going mad. And we worked our live through, planting and growing in the sympathetic soil, houses full of children, jovial uncles, precious gifts under trees.

The roads came, and the men, like the stone they were laying down, all ruthlessly glad, all obscenely familiar with their lives. My children have vanished down side streets of tomorrow never to be seen again, sending postcards of success, and I, aging, sense the subtle fissures in the bridge that I have tread to see my god.

I have not desired my madness in many years, past relative graves and highways. So long a night it has been since I have struck a blow for my own life, which is the capacity to straddle the spires of one's insanity.

I feel now that I perch like a nightmare on the breast of this good earth. All this is left for us to be is strange, malignant tumors, loathsome in towers, or skull and crossbone warnings on poison wells.

Climb that ladder, I hollered from the 7th floor window, don't stop until the clouds begin. That cat had been at my chair for 13 years without an incident, ever since old grandpa retired to a photograph. Together we have known the feel of this city on our back, we have heard the fables of the fat men, how the fields were put to death and streets were sown.

In the name of History we have slept at their feet, at odds with our heart, estranged from our flesh. Sons of miners collect refuse, sons of farmers sweep. (The streets are bright with pain, yet the nerve of the land lies still.) Our tools? These are but instruments of faith and all our labors, rituals. Take counsel of metaphysicians, that we may appease all we cannot see. Our eyes have grown dim among the details, of our curious existence...

So here we are window leapers. We are old. History is in our bone. The stone is hard beneath our feet, and we have left no place to rest, but in the legend..."

She spit all this out, then stopped abruptly, as if walled in, waking, from a dream. She sat down, and a younger person stood up.

5
Star-crossed Lovers

I chase her through the Sundays of a thousand years, candles on a large oaken table with great bowls of fruit sweating under religious lights. Deep causes in these rooms rose over sun-filled windows, casting large, lucid shadows. I told her I would hold her, secret in the ferns. I told her I would have.

She aged with pitiless rapidity, her doom gathering over her head like an outstretched, dropping net. I think that it is these buildings, which are not built for the dare. Trapped in closets, desolate, eating oranges in her imagination under a thunderstorm, painted and naked through the hidden years of her life, she marched closer. She marched through scuffles of mind and body on plush rugs, in backseats of cars, as seen from solitude windows crisscrossing like invisible wires through the armies, the gardens, and the radio, developing free-floating anxieties and demanding answers from God. She marched through the ditches and later confessed, she marched through the nunnery and through the vast, fear-filled gymnasiums, she marched through the hothouse where she wept and waited vainly for green replies...

The dare is the arc of continuance. Birds with delicate throats came to gossip with her from high ledges, twittering wisely their pastoral gossip and remedies, through the evenings and shutters. She dined alone, at regular intervals, table full of echoes, dull clatter of forks on plates. Her eyes flickered abstractedly over the furniture of her universe. Outside, unknown, machinery unwound, trucks loaded and unloaded trade secrets, busloads of people departed and returned from far-off places in the space of a few seconds. She rose from the table and blessed the world, gliding to the window where the birds called to her...over. She jumped."

He finishes, sits down, and another rises, stiffly.

The five who've spoken sit clumped together. It is a fresco. In the faces of those whose stories remain resides an unresolved charge, a tension, connected with storage of experience without modes of discharge, and something dark, indefinite dominates their features. Nevertheless, though coiled, as springs, they are calm. They visualize the girl. The moon shines in.

And these people are friends, they love each other. A marriage is taking place. A peculiar, difficult integrity binds them.

Outside a clock strikes. The one who stands is pale, with flaxen hair, and delicate features.

6

Children In A Picture

It is a picture of two children. The room in which they sit is crystalline, mounted portraits of friars, dead monarchs, decorating the walls, which are tasteful and elegant. A cat sleeps on a rug. A door stands, slightly ajar. Light shines in through the skylight. The girl on the left, with a blurry, kind face has stretched an orange string across the index fingers of her two hands, and holds it there perhaps 12 inches apart. A younger figure, either boy or girl, stares intently into the design and wets his lips with the tip of his tongue…This is what is horrible. In the background, a chandelier in the act of falling."

He looks at hem, as if expecting a reaction. Outside a clock strikes. He wants to explain but realizes he cannot, at least not yet, so sits down, and another person, young, stands up.

7

Will I Ever?

Will I ever get out of Chinatown?

Ho Chin, the galley slave, they call me. I have five brothers and six sisters, and I'm the youngest in the litter. Is there ever any quiet in our apartment? Kids sleep two to a bed. At 6 a.m., we're off to the restaurant. The working crowds pour in. It's into the back for me, washing the dishes. Pots, pans, big grease fat in the wok. I talk in my sleep, never get enough sleep.

Walk out, and see them all eating. Rushing their chopsticks into their mouths, making conversation, or on their iPhones.

Hear on the radio, "My dreams are not as empty as my conscience seems to be…"

Leave their credit cards on the table, alligator arms wait for the person next to them, to pay the bill.

They do not know what I am thinking, the kid in the

kitchen. They do not understand, or care, that I have dreams.

Every so often a pretty girl looks up shyly from her soup, and casts her face down again. For a moment our eyes meet.

My heart is in a cage, ravening like a beast, behind fragile and weary bars. I return to the kitchen and the dishes, always the dishes, piling up.

I met a girl at the library the other day, she's priceless. I call her Princess.

8

Family Matters

I am a girl in high school, coming of age in America. My skin is dark, my parents are strict. I remember streets teeming with bicycles, rickety, shambling tenements, slums stretching for miles, trash can fires in the alleys, where people cook. Our family was more fortunate, we had tea in a stucco courtyard. Now my father brings us from India to America, where he works in a computer company, in a white coat. My brothers and sisters scream, and laugh, and cry, at the table, heedless in their youth. I am the oldest child.

I have eyes for a boy. I met him in the school library. He looks so handsome, and lonesome, and forlorn.

What does skin color matter? Or where a person's from? Where they are going is what matters.

My father says he will disown me if I go out with not my kind. Stick with your own kind, he snarls. My mother echoes the party line.

I feel I am awakening in my body, my mind. I feel like I'm an alien, amid the riches in America. I watch the TV, the ads. Unlike some girls, I have self respect, do not behave cheaply. I want the best of what America has to offer. Is that so wrong?

Changes are taking place in me, that I cannot control. Only in high school now, what changes will come over me in college?

9

Café Goer

…"Sidewalk cafes in nighttimes under war-time floodlights. Planes drone overhead, dropping pamphlets of international import on heads of passersby.

The streets are thronged, full of lovers and criminals, sinister convocations of defrocked priests conversing in privileged dialects, haunted political leaders. The lame and the unknown intersect, mumbling incantations, reviewing stark personal encounters at truth tables, in the shadow of a falling bridge. News of galactic conspiracies float in on the wind, over smokers.

Those at the café dine appreciatively, quietly reflect, minds dipping into street noises from calm, emotive distances. They turn pages of papers, light cigarettes, cancer sticks. They regard the scene with interest. Men who have been accused of censoring the dawn discourse in abstruse languages from balconies, screaming down literate prophecies upon the masses. Historic moments pass, seized by angular opportunists. Bombs drop, whining. Suddenly, the entire block opposite the cafe goes up in flame. Tragedies unfold, that beg the telling. Those at the café remain seated as the table is being cleared, domed heads arched over rooflines, gazing into explosions three thousand years ago."

The fellow, himself with a domed head, sits down, calm, and impetuously, almost before he's in his chair, another begins.

10
Well-fed Adolescent

I stroll down a pleasant street for three hours, humming, turning my eyes to the incredible structures which line my sight. We admit, they are amazing, how did they get here, what does it all signify? They lean good-naturedly over my shoulder, confiding to me their astonishment at their own selves. In my mind, I pass a blind newsman, oracular, and acknowledge the signs which surround me. Windows beam, full of faces and birthdays. Subways wait impatiently underfoot.

In my mind, there is no implacability, no nightmares hatching with the authority of 200 years in the dreaming up, no labyrinths uncoiling with sorry fates, or creatures streaming within them, lost and unknown. There is no lady spinning, deceitful and secret above our heads, no shadows washing through eyes, no shades dangling from clotheslines in a consumptive rain. All shutters are thrown back, all windows look on dazzled, all minds behind eyes regard each other generously, graciously, in the animate air. The snake of our years which some are condemned to travel, solitary, fearful, under the glittering eye of our own confusion, will disappear. The men who are waiting, skull-torn, soul-wrecked, badgered into senselessness by flying clocks, heart-bent locomotives, will be picked up. Mazes will become pathways, and we will look upon one another approaching from all directions. And with our lives and loves we will return the gesture, to the luminous hands of passing time."

He sits down abruptly, and a man with a face resembling a map charting territory not often explored, rises portentously, and draws a deep breath, in out, in out.

11
Old Codger

I, who am old, gone down the alleys in an invisible jeep, yearning for combat, gone down into the mines of invisible forces to call their bluffs, gone in trucks and horses, carriages, lone feet advancing out of sight and out of mind, to places few have ever been, and what joy did they hold anyway, I who watch the colors come and go, brief flickers of old movies, watch the people pass, watch the cars zoom out of my life, the trailers on the highways, searching, I, who have eyes, say it is easy to survive, as the planets turn and the sun continues it is easy.

For each of us longs to be as the sun which shines, unquestionable and superb, who knows itself fully by those bodies which surround it, in acknowledgment, in obeisance, establishing themselves devoutly in its fire, drawing nearer so as to share in its everlastingness. Each man or woman is their own sun, and by those who revolve around them, by those are they separated from the soulless blue void, original heart-fear. In this embroilment, this multi-fold ravel, resides our sanity. Networks, covenants, forms of contract keep us distant from our frights, ancient uneases, all entanglement obscures from us our essential lonely blueness, strange mishap of I-hood, situated weirdly.

Green trees sway robustly in the breeze. The flowers lean to light. The flat leaves waken. And yet to we, who are passion past flames, eye beyond desire, are not there suns beyond these suns? Or perhaps not. All life is exposure, the secret at the heart of things strains to day, desiring publicity. The windows open, to what musty sights of ragged webs, to what clarities which we have never dreamed, a new day on earth."

With eyes glowing like embers, he sits down. Once again, the clock strikes. Only one remains. With diffidence, as if making a difficult decision, and still not sure of its standing in his own mind, he rises.

12

A Sailor Tells A Tale

With my mind full of old mythologies I have paced my room, anxious for myself, irritable with deep irritations, few friends, few kinsmen, or a heart fireplace to arm my thoughts. Around and around I go, evoking memories older than my body, open to imbue it, sorrowful though it may be.

I too have become entwined, and transfused into this world, dispersed, made unnameable many currents, to work, to produce, driven with breaths no longer mine. Or am I a sailor on an imaginary sea, caught in my own picture, adrift?

We twelve, see how we sit here, as if we were the ghostly months of the years themselves that pass by our large windows, raining gray tears down. See how we still cling, observing the youth who stands before us, observing ourselves, hoping past hope, raw eyes and tender ears aching to be burned.

Why do we feel wretched breathing here? Wretched in body, wretched in spirit. Wretched under the sky in an old blue refrigerator, we are a warning, we need warming.

Oh Lord, I have lost confidence in the work of my hands. Why won't the stars live up to my dreams?

He falls silent. A clock strikes, then fades away. All twelve sway together, for a moment, in time.

1

It is past dawn when the twelve disperse. The youth gazes out upon an adjacent building, tall and steep as the one he is buried in. For a brief moment, as if his eyes were cast upon a screen, he sees clearly before him the image of a place where he has never been. Under a roof of spreading trees, leaves blither down like snowflakes, mutable and orange under an elevate sun.

127

In the morning the twelve will make a trek out to the lake, at the edge of the city. He thinks, what matter that time goes by and some hides in my hair? What matter the breadth of the sky, under which all men fit? And he saw the lake before him, deep and secret, and he accepted the morrow when the germ of his own body would be released into the lake.

2

A large mirror of water under a quiet afternoon. The sun hangs a drop of blood in mid-sky, as if suspended from a dropper. Great white birds wheel overhead in high, tight circles. White sands glitter across the day.

Through the outstretched, crystalline expanse the twelve approach, in wagons, carts, on foot. They arranged the picaresque this way. The mysteriously emergent youth follows a short distance back. Behind them, like a boa, stretches the record of their journey to the borders of this lake, where the water gleams, ancient and deathless. They stand where the water begins, and look across its surface. Clouds drift by. Faint sounds of machinery waft in on the wind, fore and aft.

They think perhaps of their city. Or their childhood, under this sun, and the years which in one stroke they would attempt to be done with. They think of grace, and whether grace lives for human's sake, or whether it vanishes with the fruitful sky.

They immerse, immense. On a mid-summer afternoon in the country, twelve figures look out, then back to a boy, who motions them forward. Following his gesture, they lean over and regard themselves in the water, blurry and golden, disrupted by a sudden breeze. The youth moves up to join them. On a mid-summer afternoon in the country, birds cry out, and the sky dims, dark as an old masterpiece. Back among those buildings clocks strike, but here time is suspended. On a mid-summer afternoon in the country, no one speaks as they disrobe, wade out, farther and farther into the accepting water.

5
No Way Out

They sit looking at each other. They've finished their meals chain restaurant red tables plateglass the traffic outside snarled cool remote blue sky.

"I'm going to start going to church. I'm going to start going to their extra-curricular activities."

The chunky blond woman of 24 throws back her shoulders, shakes her blond hair, stares into the eyes of her husky black companion. He stares back, one eyebrow raised skeptically.

"I am. I'm going to. I'm sick of work. Arranging phonebooks alphabetically." She pauses, looks forlorn. "I hate work. I'm stuck in a chair eight hours straight. When I leave I feel fat. And Doug don't like fat women. He's been talking to you about me, hasn't he? What's he been saying? Has he been putting me down? Just cause I don't keep in shape? Tell me. You're his friend, he talks to you. Has he been complaining?"

Her companion says nothing. He looks at her steadily, sending waves of hostility and contempt.

"What's Doug been saying? You're his friend. Tell me."

Arthur, her companion, hesitates. "Nothing baby. Nothing at all. You think he's talking?"

"I don't think, I know. Cause I'm getting fat. He's told me. 'Baby,' he says, 'if you get fat, I get out.'"

A young mother with a baby walks in, the baby sucking on a bottle. The mother, drawn, orders a hamburger, the baby starts crying loudly, she abruptly departs, leaving the waitress holding her hamburger, cursing.

"I'm getting fat. I don't deny it," the girl was saying. "Doug, he don't always treat me so nice, you know. Not like he used to, anyway. I been bored.

So I get fat. But you're his friend. You don't care about me one way or the other."

"I care about you , baby."

Arthur looks out the window, suppressing an unpleasant smirk, which goes, however, unnoticed, in his companion's distraught, unnerved state. Growing fat is obsessing her, to an unheard-of degree. She worries constantly. She suddenly puts on weight, visibly, right in front of his eyes.

"I can't believe it baby. Something's happening to you." He tips a chair, pushing backward, to escape her. "Catch you some other time. Good talking to you."

She sees herself in the restaurant-window reflected. Traffic goes by outside.

"If only my job were different. If only Doug were nicer like he used to be. If only...I need a vacation or something. Maybe I'll go to church Sunday. It will be like when Mama used to take me."

As she is getting up to leave, her lover Doug walks past the window, sees her, and hurries quickly away. She would know his black face anywhere. Still...maybe it wasn't.

"I don't know... I just don't know. It seems so long ago I was a little girl going to church. We'd sit in the middle row, the preacher would give a sermon, and the congregation would be so quiet and respectful. Then after the sermon we'd eat and talk. It's like a lifetime ago."

She sighs. Her face droops down, is sweaty.

"Doug would never take me. He'd just laugh. Arthur got up so fast as if he were scared. Was that Doug passed by just now? Well, really, I'm not so fat, am I?"

But as she turns and walks towards the door, all eyes are on her, she feels them, and her eyes look in the plateglass. Her body has expanded so much she has to excuse herself squeezing through aisles big enough for two ordinary people, and the scrape of chairs pushing in to let her by is deafening. "I don't know. I don't know what it is," she thinks to herself. "I'm going to start going to church."

Her shoulders, barely narrow enough to fit through, fill the door. As she wriggles through, she is under the impression traffic has stopped to look at her. "They're watching me," she thinks, cringing. She sees Doug walking the other way, whispering and laughing, with Arthur, suddenly, and with a woman on his arm she doesn't know. Her heart sinks. Strangers stare. Her lover is deserting her.

She walks out, feeling suddenly ill. Her world crumbles, she's aware with piercing clarity she will continue, she will get fatter, it's a process, it won't stop. She looks up, over the traffic. A word hangs, over the city, the word 'FAT.' She winces, walks on, blocks unwind, remote cold sky.

However, she recovers. "My job's not so bad, and even if I don't have Doug, there are other things," she reasons. "I can start church."

134

She straightens herself up. She walks on. It's a beautiful day and by the time she goes into another chain restaurant for a milkshake she is humming.